DEAD
LEAVES

Boo Books

DEAD
LEAVES

Andrew David Barker

Published by
Boo Books
32 Westbury Street
Derby
DE22 3PN

Dead Leaves Copyright © 2015 Andrew David Barker

Cover Designed by Amanda Plant © 2015

Typesetting by
handebooks.co.uk

Printed by
Biddles

ISBN 978-0-9927285-8-8

AUTHOR'S NOTE

I have taken many liberties in telling this tale. The history of the Video Nasty – the media furore of moral panic and outrage – is a complex one. It was a firestorm which lasted many years in the UK – though it was at its most fervent from 1982 to 1984 – and, it could be argued, stretched well into the late nineties.

However, for the purposes of this story, I have condensed much of its long and strange history into a single October in 1983: newspaper headlines, news readers and MPs I may have quoted won't necessarily have been printed or spoken during the specific time frame of this story.

Anyone interested in the 'moral panic' surrounding these films during the early eighties should check out Jake West's excellent documentaries on the subject, Video Nasties: Moral Panic, Censorship & Videotape, *and its sequel,* Draconian Days.

I have also taken liberties in the story's setting – that of my hometown of Derby. Several of the pubs and clubs mentioned may not have been open in the October of 1983, but again, I have bent the truth for the purposes of my story.

I would like to thank Leigh Dovey, Rishi Thaker, David Flint, Matthew Waldram and especially Gary Dalkin for advice, pointers and editorial guidance in the writing of this book. I'd also like to thank Simon Clark for his unending support and encouragement.

Andrew David Barker, August 2015

For me mum and dad

1.

'Seen this?'

Paul thrust a copy of *Nightmare in a Damaged Brain* into my hand. The cover showed a decidedly distraught man crying tears of blood, whilst holding – what I could only assume to be – the eponymous damaged brain.

'No,' I said.

'Ah man, behind the times or what!'

We were stood in Ray's Video Emporium; a cramped, narrow little shop stacked wall-to-wall with thrillingly lurid video boxes. This was our Mecca in the autumn of 1983 – a place of unfathomable visions of extreme violence and unrelenting mayhem. What kid could ask for more?

Paul picked up another video box.

'What about this one?'

It was *Cannibal Ferox*.

'Nope,' I said.

'Jesus, Scott, you seen anything?'

'I guess not,' I said, a little testily.

I'd known Paul since school and he was, by his own estimation, the ultimate gorehound. His was a steady diet of dismemberment, disembowelment and the shuffling, decaying dead. He'd watch that stuff while he was having his tea and not think anything of it. A fact which he was most proud of.

'This one?' he asked, holding up a copy of *The Burning*.

'Not yet.'

Paul shook his head in disapproval.

The Emporium's proprietor, Ray Ellis – a man after Paul's heart – was something of a connoisseur when it came to the more extreme videos on the market. If you wanted to rent, say, *Smokey and the Bandit* or *Flash Gordon*, then you went across town to Video Magic, but if you wanted tits and gore, you went to Ray's.

Yet so cramped was the Emporium that any more than three or four patrons at any given time would be enough to cause major congestion, severely putting into question the shop's overtly grandiose name (that day, however, there was only myself and Paul in the place).

Ray – a gangly, emaciated looking bloke – would sit behind a small counter at the back of the shop, chain-smoking and, more often than not, reading a paperback – if it wasn't Shaun Hutson, then it was Guy N. Smith; all killer slugs and giant crabs – and he'd offer up recommendations for the latest blood-soaked title for our delectation. Behind Ray were stacks and stacks of video tapes, all labelled alphabetically, while beneath the counter were his collection of off-the-shelf 'blueys'. The only one of us who'd rented one of those had been Mark, but then, he was eighteen, a year older than either myself or Paul, and also the only one of us to have an actual girlfriend – or a job for that matter. I suppose he was the closest thing to an actual grown up in our gang. (Mark told us that he'd talked his girlfriend, Lindsay, into watching Ray's porno with him, only to find that it was about some guy dressed up in a gorilla suit going around getting blowies off 'dog-rough women', as he put it. Apparently, Lindsay had not been impressed, to say the least.)

Paul shoved *Tenebrae* into my hand. 'You've gotta have seen this one?'

'No.'

'Jesus Christ! It's fucking Argento, man.'

'Well, you seen *Last House on the Left* yet?' I retorted.

'Fuckin' do one.'

I knew that would get him. It was the bane of his existence that I'd seen *Last House* and he hadn't.

Ray looked at us from over his paperback – currently James Herbert's *The Fog* – and smiled a mouth full of yellow-stained teeth. 'What you boys lookin' for this time?'

'Dunno,' said Paul, clearly still sulking from the *Last House* comment.

'Well,' I interjected, 'that's not strictly true, is it, Paul?'

'No?'

'No. There is a film we've been after for ages.'

'Fucksake,' muttered Paul. 'Don't keep going on about bleeding *Last House on the Left* will ya.'

'Not *Last House*, you div. What's the film we're always talking about?'

Paul shrugged. I sighed.

'*The Evil Dead*,' I offered.

'Oh. Right. Yeah. That looks well wicked.'

'I know, you bellend. We've talked about it loads.'

Paul stared at me gone out, then he blinked and somewhere inside that head of his, a light bulb flickered.

The Evil Dead, billed as the "ultimate experience in gruelling terror", had become the Holy Grail of must-see-videos within our small circle (even if Paul had momentary lapsed in this regard). Not one of us had seen it, but boy, had we read about it. At least, I had.

Every *Fangoria* article, every review, and every interview with the filmmakers I could find I pored over with feverish eyes. Stephen King, no less, had called it "The most ferociously original horror film of the year" and the few people I'd met who had seen it claimed it was the most balls-to-the-wall scary movie they'd ever watched. To a seventeen-year-old gorehound in the making, this film couldn't have ticked any more boxes if it tried.

'*Evil Dead*, hey…' muttered Ray Ellis. He relit the fag end hanging out his mouth, then put his bookmark (a playing card) inside *The Fog* and hid it away beneath the counter – where it presumably sat on top of a stack of blueys. 'That's one hell of a film,' he continued. 'Pretty hard to get hold of.'

'Tell me about it,' I said. 'We've been after it ages.'

'I had my copy nicked not long ago,' he said, blowing smoke out through his nose.

'Nicked?' said Paul.

'Yeah. It's *very* sought after.'

'That good, is it?' Paul's eyes were gleaming.

'It's a fucking film and a half, my friend. But that's not the only reason for its rarity.'

'No?' I said.

'No. It was in the papers again this morning. The powers that be in this merry old land of ours don't want you to see it.'

'You mean… all that video nasty stuff on the news?' said Paul.

I think that was the first time I heard anyone say 'video nasty'. At that age, I was pretty much oblivious to most things going on in the world. My life was filled with nothing but horror movies, drinking, Pink Floyd and looking at, but very rarely talking to, girls. I hardly ever watched the news, and the tabloids were for Page 3 and Page 3 alone.

'Yeah,' said Ray, clearing his throat. 'In fact, a lot of the titles in this very shop are highly sought after. Especially by the filth.' He seemed quite proud of this. 'There's gonna be a massive crackdown soon,' he added.

'What do you mean?' I asked.

Ray looked at me for a moment, crushed his butt into an ashtray, then immediately lit another fag. He took a lungful, then said, 'I've heard they've started raiding shops up in Manchester. It's only a matter of time...'

'What, video shops?' said Paul.

'Yeah. Took all this fella's stock and locked him up.'

'In jail?' I said. 'For what?'

'For possessing *obscene material*, or so the papers said.'

'But,' Paul began. 'They're just films.'

'I couldn't agree more,' said Ray.

We all fell silent. I absentmindedly picked up the box for *Halloween II* and looked at the pictures on the back cover. That one I had seen.

I felt troubled by what Ray had told us, but also, I was annoyed at my own ignorance. I knew nothing of a major crackdown by 'the powers-that-be' on the very films I loved so much, and the thought of someone going to prison for simply trading such videos unnerved and confused me.

Ray came from behind the counter and walked up to us. His skin was loose on his bones, his eyes like black beads.

'You wanna copy of *Evil Dead?*'

'Yeah,' Paul and I replied in unison.

'I know a guy, who knows a guy... who knows a guy who *might* have a copy. But it'll cost you.'

'How much?' I asked.

'Sixty quid.'

'Fucking bollocks,' spat Paul.

'Look, it's not a rental. You'd be buyin' it. It would be yours. To keep.'

I looked at Paul. He just shrugged his shoulders at me.

I said, 'You're on.'

'Good stuff,' said Ray of Ray's Video Emporium. 'Be back here tomorrow. With the money.'

2.

'Where the hell are we going to get sixty quid from?'

Paul lay on the grass, shielding his eyes against the sun. I was sat beside him, snapping twigs in half. We were down at the weir – a usual haunt – and were happily idling by the rushing water for the fourth day in a row. It was October and the low sun illuminated the browns and reds and golds, making the world look like a painting. It was bright, though not particularly warm, but at least it was dry. It had rained throughout September and it'd been one hell of a long, miserable month (not least because my parents had constantly badgered me about getting a job). Then, into October, the clear autumn sun came. It felt like the last gasp of a long ago summer and we certainly made the most of it; Paul and I that is. We were never home.

Paul shoved me. 'Well? Come on, Scott, it was your bright idea…'

'Mark's working ain't he,' I said. 'He might have a few bob he could lend us.'

'I doubt he'd go for that, mate. Not sixty squidlers anyway.'

'Well, what if we all threw in, like… twenty quid apiece?'

Paul sighed. 'Scott, I can't even spare a fiver at the minute. I don't sign on till next week.'

We fell silent. I watched the river rush down through the weir. There was something soothing about it. I could also hear the steady hum of traffic from the dual carriageway across the water; unseen, but very much present.

I turned to Paul, 'What about your brother?'

'No way.'

'Why? He got you into horror movies, didn't he? He'd understand.'

'He's changed big time.'

'Seems all right to me.'

'Well you don't have to live with him, do you?'

'I guess not. But just because he's in the police now don't mean he's any different.'

'Really? The dipshit's well changed. Thinks he's all better than us 'un everythin'. Even me dad thinks he's a knob.'

5

'I don't think that's true.'

'What do you fucking know? Carl's a right spaz.'

'Look, all I'm sayin' is… I reckon he might lend us the money, or at least throw in. I mean, he's a massive horror fan, ain't he?'

'Just drop it, alright. I ain't askin' Carl.'

'Fine,' I said, and fell silent.

Asking Paul if his brother would front the money was indeed a long shot, but I was already clutching at straws. Truth was, I'd known back at the Video Emporium that it would be nigh-on impossible for us to get our hands on that amount of money, especially at such short notice. But there was no way I was going to pass up on Ray's offer. Not just like that. I had to see *The Evil Dead*. There had to be a way.

3.

I'd begun 1983 in a different place altogether – both in circumstance and cinemology. At the beginning of the year I was still in school – just about to completely fuck up my O-Levels – never giving a moment's thought as to what I'd do once I left in July. My film obsessions at that time were all spearheaded by George Lucas. *Return of the Jedi* was released in the May of that year and I'd been there, like a loyal dog, on opening day. I went to see it at the Trocadero in town with Mark and a younger lad named Sam. We queued for nearly two hours to get in.

I remember buzzing off the film initially – I loved all the stuff in Jabba's Palace at the start and the final lightsaber duel between Luke and Vader – but the more I thought about it over the next few days, the more I realised two things: *Jedi* was no *Empire*, but moreover, a shift had occurred in me; *Star Wars* no longer held all the cards; its appeal had diminished. I now wanted something harder.

Two weeks later I got that very thing when I saw *Dawn of the Dead* round at Paul's house.

4.

Throughout May and June we were sitting our O-Levels and supposedly studying hard. Except very little studying was actually undertaken on my part. I just drifted into exams, wrote down a few half-hearted answers to questions I barely read, then drifted out again. Nights were filled with either hanging out down the graveyard – drinking cheap beer and talking about girls – or piling round someone's bedroom to listen to Floyd or Maiden (those two bands were pretty much on a loop back then), and then ultimately throwing on a film.

I saw *Dawn of the Dead* on June 1st (yes, I even remember the date), after an evening of drinking down the park. I'd gone back to Paul's house to borrow a copy of Stephen King's *Night Shift* (I only tended to read short stories back then) on Paul's own recommendation. He was always jabbering on about something or another, be it a book or a record. Mostly it'd be a film though; Paul could talk them up no end. He'd already given me the full M.O. on George A. Romero in the weeks before and had pretty much laid out every grisly detail of both *Night* and *Dawn* several times over. Yet, even though Paul had given away much of the plot (and gore, of course), actually sitting there watching it was still an absolute assault on the senses. There were no Ewoks in Pittsburgh; I'd found a new George.

Before then, the only horror films I'd been exposed to were the old Hammers that tended to play on television late on a Friday night, and, with the exception of the TV miniseries of *Salem's Lot* (which had scared me rigid, I have to admit), that was it. So watching *Dawn of the Dead* pinned me to the wall and rattled me for days. After that I was more or less on a strict diet of gore. And with the boom of the video market, there was no better time to be a burgeoning horror fan.

5.

I first read about *The Evil Dead* in an issue of *Starburst* magazine over that summer. According to the article, the film contained, among other things, something called Candarian demons, unprecedented bodily dismemberment and, to top all that, trees that rape. All by three kids from Michigan who'd raised the money by convincing lawyers and dentists and the like to invest in their project. The film's writer/director, Sam Raimi, wasn't much older than myself (barely twenty when he started production in 1979), and his two partners, actor/producer Bruce Campbell and producer Rob Tapert, were only a few years older than that.

This was a revelation. I'd always thought of films as being made by established veterans who'd gotten into the business either through heritage and/or by their proximity to Hollywood. Movies were something *other people* got to make, not kids from the back of beyond. The idea that these guys went out to a cabin in Tennessee and came back with the most original and ferocious horror film in years blew my tiny little mind. It was punk rock.

It was the seed that sowed my future.

6.

From across the dinner table my dad placed the local paper under my nose. He'd circled a job vacancy in blue pen. It read:

**Warehouse Picker & Packer
Permanent Vacancy for enthusiastic and
committed warehouse operative.
Must be hardworking and able to communicate
effectively as part of a team.**

That's as far as I read, yet I continued to stare at the page, feigning interest. The words *Permanent Vacancy* scared the shit out of me.

'Well?' said my dad.

'Yeah,' I returned, with all the enthusiasm I could muster – which was to say, very little.

'I want you to ring them first thing in the morning and get an application form filled out.'

I shoved a few chips into my mouth.

'Your dad's right,' said my mum, cleaning up gravy from her plate with a slice of bread. 'This isn't the summer holidays anymore, Scott. It's nearly November and you really need to start thinking seriously about your future.'

'It's just…' I began, swallowing hard.

'It's just what?' said me dad.

'It's just… I've been thinking… about applying to go to film school.'

'Film school! What the hell is film school?'

'It's where you go to learn how to make films, Dad.'

'There's a school for that?'

'Yes.'

'Where?'

'London.'

'Brilliant. And how are you going to afford to live down there, Mr. Spielberg?'

'Well…' I faulted. I hadn't thought about that minor detail.

Mum chimed in. 'And how much does this course cost, Scott?'

'I'm not sure. Erm. About three thousand pounds, I think.'

'Three grand!' said Dad.

'That's over three years,' I offered.

'So you want to go to London for three years to learn how to make films?'

'Yeah.'

'And what happens then?'

'What do you mean?'

'I mean, once you've finished this amazing course and you've learned how to point a camera at a load of dozy actors...'

'Well, I'll make a film, won't I.'

'Really? I can just imagine one of your films, Scott.'

'What does that mean?'

'Look, you need to buck your ideas up, lad. Life isn't one big holiday camp. By the time I was your age I had three jobs. You need to pull your socks up and straighten yoursen out.'

'Your dad's right, Scott,' Mum said. 'It's time to start thinking like a grown up. I mean, really... film school? Scott, films aren't made by people like us. You need money to do that and live in America. No one from the Midlands has ever gone into the movies. It's ridiculous.'

I knew that wasn't true, but I didn't have the strength to argue.

7.

After dinner, the Pirate Man visited our household. His real name was Colin, but he was known as the Pirate Man to Dad and me. He was a grubby little man in an ill-fitting suit and broken shoes, who carried with him a suitcase full of video tapes – pirated video tapes to be precise, hence the moniker.

Dad would have him round once in a while to build on his already extensive library of VHS treasures. You see, Dad may have got on my back about work and money and such, but our love of films was always something we could bond over. Dad liked sci-fi films and westerns and the odd war film (not to mention blueys – although he thought I didn't know about those). He also loved Laurel & Hardy, and we'd often roll about watching them while mum sat po-faced and disdainful, which, of course, only made it funnier.

Dad had embraced the video age with gusto, being one of the first people round our way to own a video player (he told me years later that it cost £500 and took him three years to pay off). A great bulky thing is was too, with long, talon-like buttons, a glorious top-loading compartment which looked so futuristic and cool that I kept ejecting tapes just to watch it open, and if that wasn't enough, a remote control on a wire. The day it arrived in our house – which may have been the Christmas of 1982, or a little earlier – was the day my obsession with movies went into overdrive. No more waiting for a film to come on at the Trocadero, or hoping in vain that they'd put something cool on TV. No. Now we had films on tap, and that hulking, almost dangerous looking machine became the centre of my entire universe.

Dad got most of his films from the Pirate Man, never having the time nor the inclination to go to a video shop and rent them. As always, Dad invited Colin into the front room where there was enough floor space to open up that most hallowed suitcase and reveal its sacred wonders.

Dad put the big light on. 'What new ones you got?'

Colin rubbed his chin and said, 'What haven't I got, Ian. You name it, I've probably got it.'

Dad riffled through. All the tapes were unboxed, only

identifiable by sticky labels scrawled in Colin's almost illegible handwriting.

'What's this one like?' asked my dad, holding a particular tape up to Colin.

'Yeah, that's a goodun. Right up your street.' He grinned.

Dad grunted and put the tape to one side. I looked over and deciphered the handwriting: *I Spit on your Grave.*

Dad spied another. '*Soldier Blue...* What a film! I'll have that.'

He put that tape to the side also.

'It's not cut to ribbons is it?'

Colin frowned. 'What's that?'

'*Soldier Blue.*'

'No, no. Uncut, Ian. In all its glory.'

Dad continued on, putting aside *The New Barbarians, SS Experiment Camp, Cut-Throats Nine* and something called *Black Liquorice and Sweet White Cream*, which I imagined would be hidden away in his cardboard upstairs.

'How much for all these then, Col?'

Colin thought about it for a moment, then said, 'Err. A ton.'

'Fucking bollocks, Col. That's nearly twenty quid a tape.'

'That's the going rate now.'

'But surely buying in bulk...'

I butted in. 'You got *The Evil Dead,* Colin?'

The Pirate Man whistled through his teeth. 'That's a real goodun, that one.'

'You got it then?' I said, unable to contain my excitement.

'Did have. Sold a copy just last week, and then my master got all chewed up. Devastated.' He turned to my dad, 'And that one went for thirty quid, Ian.'

'Never heard of it,' said Dad.

'Could you get hold of another copy?' I asked.

'Dunno. Maybe. That one gets snapped up pretty quick.'

I turned to Dad. 'Instead of getting all these, how about you just get two, and then I can use the rest of the money and get us a copy of *The Evil Dead.*'

'What the fucking hell you talking about, lad?' Dad would always swear in front of me when mum wasn't around.

I glanced at Colin. He was giving me a very stony look.

'It's just… Ray down at the video shop said he can get us copy, but he wants, like, sixty pounds.'

'Sixty quid for a video!'

'Yeah, but it's really hard to get hold of, Dad. It's supposed to be amazing. Like the best horror film ever.'

I looked at Colin, hoping he would confirm this, but he gave me nothing, other than a bona fide death stare.

'So, let me get this straight,' said Dad. 'You want me to *not* buy these films – films *I* want – but instead give you the money to go and buy some poxy tape that *you* want?'

'Erm. Yeah.' My voice had suddenly become very small.

'Honestly, if your brains were dynamite, boy, you wouldn't have enough to blow ya hat off.'

'But, Dad…'

'I've got three words for you, Scott.'

'What?' I asked, knowing full well that the words in question were in no way going to be good.

'Get. A. Job.'

Colin sniggered.

'You get a job, Scott, and you can buy all the films you want. After you've paid me some rent, of course.'

Colin gave a hearty belly laugh.

8.

Later that night, I met Paul and Mark down at the graveyard. Mark had brought along his customary beers and had his arse parked on a gravestone, can in hand. Paul was stood, guzzling his own can, half cut in a long slice of moonlight. They both looked extremely shady as I approached. Once they saw it was me, however, their guilty-as-charged faces reverted to their usual mask of casual indifference.

'Alright, Bradley' said Mark. He usually called me by my last name. 'Here.' He bent down, picked up a can and handed it to me.

'Cheers.' I cracked it open and took a swig.

Paul stepped in and closed the circle. 'I was just telling Mark about your fail today at Ray's.'

'It wasn't a fail.'

'Wasn't it? So you've got the sixty quid you promised Ray then?'

'Well, no, but...'

'There you go then.'

I took another long gulp. The night was clear, but cold. My fingers were freezing holding the can and I had to keep swapping it from one hand to the other. I noticed Paul was doing the same. A breeze kicked up, sibilantly scattering dead leaves among the headstones. Above, the moon was a real graveyard moon, fat and waxing, illuminating the night from a veil of wispy black clouds. It was certainly October.

'How's work?' I asked Mark, trying to break the silence (and change the subject).

'Wank.'

'Yeah?'

'Yeah. Fucking dreading winter. It's bad enough now. I get up in the dark; I come home in the dark. Only daylight I see is on a fucking building site. It's grim, mate.'

'Sounds it. You still working in Belper?'

'Yeah. In the van at half six every morning. I've got a mix out before you two fuckers are probably even out of bed.'

'There's no probably about it,' said Paul. 'I didn't get up today until half ten.'

'Do one.'

I knocked back the last dregs from my can and then threw it to the ground.

'Have another?' I asked Mark.

'Sure. You know what scares the shit outta me?'

'What?' I said, cracking open the can.

'These old boys on the trowel have been doing it since they left school. One of 'em – Les – he's sixty-eight and still on the line. That's fifty fucking years, man. Day in, day out, laying brick after bastard brick.'

'Jesus,' I said.

'Too right. I can't have that.'

'Yeah but, you don't have to stay in that job, do you?' I said.

'That's what them old boys thought as well. Les told me he'd planned to go to tech and train to be an engineer or summat… then he turned round one day and he was thirty… then he was forty, and before he knew it he'd spent his entire fucking life on the trowel. Only time the poor fucker had off from bricklaying was getting shot at by Nazis.'

'That's bollocks,' said Paul.

'Why is it?' Mark was frowning.

'If he hated bricklaying so much surely he would've done summat about it years ago.'

'How do you fucking know?'

'Well, why stay in a job you fucking hate?'

'Because people have mortgages, Paul. Kids and families to support.'

'Well I wouldn't stay in a job I hated.'

'You've never even had a job.'

'I had a paper round.'

'You taking the piss? Fucking paper round. Prick. Bet you don't even pay any rent at home, do ya?'

'Yeah. Mum takes £20 out me giro every fortnight.'

'Well whoopee-fucking-doo.'

Paul's face dropped.

'I have to pay thirty quid a week, Paul. That's almost half me wages. And me dad wanted more, but I managed to talk him round. You've got it all to come, mate. You both have. Fucking wake up.'

That shit me up. I looked at the moon and wondered

where I'd be in a year's time: in the same situation as Mark? Stuck in a job I hated. My stomach knotted. The breeze kicked up the leaves again and I threw my second can to the ground.

9.

We finished off the beers and wandered the streets for a while. Talk, thankfully, moved away from the subject of work and drifted back to films, then, somehow, got onto the latest Iron Maiden album, *Piece of Mind*. All three of us agreed that 'The Trooper' was an all-time classic. Mark told us that he and Lindsay had tried to get tickets to see them in Nottingham, but the gig had sold out.

We passed our old school, kicking at the gates as we went. I looked to the main block, dark and silent in the October night. I'd spent five years of my life in that place, and now it was over and I was expected to *grow up*.

Since leaving school at the beginning of summer, it seemed not a day had gone by when I wasn't reminded of the fact that I needed to get a job. If it wasn't my parents on at me, it was Paul's mum, and if it wasn't Paul's mum, it was Lindsay. Now even Mark was getting in on the act.

You've got it all to come.

And none of them, particularly my parents, realised that the more they went on about work, the less I actually wanted to do anything about it.

Although I'd remained quiet back at the graveyard, I was kind of with Paul on the whole *why stay in a job you fucking hate* argument. Why would that old boy spend his entire life bricklaying when he claimed to hate it? It made little sense to me. And yet, I had been troubled by Mark's rationale: You get a job and life comes hurtling along; wife, kids, a nice fat mortgage; car, tax, gas and leccie bills, and fucking washing machines, and just like that, you're trapped for life. Now that did scare the shit out of me.

10.

The Silver Ghost public house was the kind of dive only fit for hardened alcoholics, pill poppers, glue sniffers, the occasional crack head and the Derby Lunatic Fringe, or D-L-F, who specialized in football violence and the odd bit of causal GBH off the terraces. Paul and I would certainly have never gone in usually, but as we passed our old school, Mark mentioned that he knew a regular in there who might be able to help us acquire a copy of *The Evil Dead*. 'Acquire' had been the word Mark had used and he didn't elaborate.

'So how do you know this guy?' Paul asked as we approached the Ghost.

'Worked with him on that job in Normanton. He's a plasterer.'

'A plasterer? How's he gonna help us?'

'Look, just trust us, will ya. And don't go shooting your mouth off in there, Paul. This is not the place to be *you*.'

Paul looked at me with a *what-the-fuck?* expression and I said, 'He means you're a bellend, but try and pretend like you're not a bellend, yeah?'

'Yeah, well funny, spunk splat.'

11.

As we entered the pub the strains of 'Hi Ho Silver Lining' trickled from the tinny speakers that bookended the bar. I hated that song. All the house lights were up bright, and pretty much every eye in the place turned in our direction. Mark took the lead and approached the bar; Paul and I followed.

The floor was sticky underfoot. A rail-thin bloke in beat up Doc Martens and a stone-washed denim jacket watched me from along the bar. His hair was peroxide and close cropped. His stare inferred that he wanted me dead. I avoided all eye contact.

'Hi Ho Silver Lining' gave way to the Sweet's 'Wig-Wam Bam' and Mark walked up to a stocky chap at the end of the bar.

'Alright, Bazza.'

Bazza turned, pint in hand. 'Well, bugger me, if it isn't the fairy. Fuck you doin' in here?'

'Oh, just nipped in for a couple, y'know.'

'Really?'

'Yeah.'

'And who are these two? Your bum chums?'

Mark forced a laugh. 'Nah, this is me mates, Paul and Scott.'

Bazza grunted in our general direction and then gulped down the remainder of his pint. He shouted over to the barman, who was currently serving the peroxide knucklehead at the other end of the bar. 'Same again, Alan. When you're ready.'

The barman shouted back, 'Righto, Barry.'

I glanced over and saw Peroxide was still staring at me. I quickly looked away.

Bazza turned his attention back to Mark. 'Where you working now?'

'Belper. Big house extension.'

'Les and Jonesy still with ya?'

'The flashing blades? Yeah, they're still going at it.'

'You not on the trowel yet then, lad?'

'Yeah, I've run in a few courses here and there. Les has shown me a bit.'

'He's a goodun is old Les. Proper lad.'

Alan came over with Bazza's pint and I risked another glance across the bar. Peroxide was still staring at me. I became incredibly interested in the spilt beer and nub ends on the floor.

'You fairies drinking or what then?' Bazza inquired. The barman, Alan, stood, arms folded, awaiting an answer.

Mark looked at Paul and me, but with both our pockets eternally hollow, we just gave a shrug. Mark sighed. 'You two are fucking useless.' He turned to the barman and said, 'Three halves of lager please, mate.'

Bazza nearly spat out his drink. 'Three halves of lager! You benders or what?'

Alan snorted.

'I mean... three pints,' said Mark, through gritted teeth. He turned to us, 'You owe me.'

'Course,' said Paul.

'Yeah, sure,' I said. 'Cheers.'

Alvin Stardust's 'My Coo-ca-Choo' rattled into action. Peroxide was still staring. I wanted to crawl in a hole.

'So, Bazza,' said Mark. 'You know how sometimes you can get your hands on videos and such. You know, from time to time, like.'

'Yeah?'

'Well, we were wondering if you could get hold of a particular tape for us?'

'Like what?'

'Like...'

'That's £2.55,' said Alan, lining the bar with three pints of the flattest looking lager you could ever wish to see. It actually looked like piss. Mark dug into his pocket and pulled out a handful of change. He counted it out, being infuriatingly slow about it. Finally he handed over the money and Alan snatched it away without a word. I glanced over at Peroxide and for once he wasn't staring at me. He was deep in conversation with a fat lad in a far-too-tight Union Jack t-shirt with an equally fetching teardrop tattoo beneath his right eye. A lad so riddled in clichés it bordered on parody.

They both turned and looked at me.

Mark took a drink, then said to Bazza, 'I want a copy of a film called *The Evil Dead*. Reckon you could get it.'

'Got that one in the back of the van, lad.'

'What?' said Mark, astonished. 'Where's your van?'

'Outside.'

Paul looked at me, smiling his head off, then knocked back his pint.

12.

Out in the pub car park we all stood huddled round the back of Bazza's van. The name of his one-man-band business was crudely painted across the back doors: MASTER PLASTER: Barry Metcalfe, then his phone number. This was repeated on both sides of the van.

The master plasterer himself was rummaging around in the back of said van, sorting through a fat bag of videotapes. He kept muttering to himself and occasionally farting. Paul and I had a hard time stifling the giggles. Only Mark's steel gaze stopped us from cracking up completely.

Finally Bazza shifted his considerable bulk around and held up a tape. 'Bingo,' he said, then practically fell out the back of the van. He righted himself and thrust the tape into Mark's hand. 'There you go,' he said, then spat and added, 'That'll be a tenner.'

Paul shot me a look and I broke into a grin. I couldn't help it. Ten pounds for *The Evil Dead* felt like the bargain of a lifetime. But then Mark said, 'Hang on,' and I felt my euphoria jolt. 'This isn't *Evil Dead*,' he continued. 'This is *Night of the Living Dead*.'

Euphoria crashed and burned.

'Yeah,' said Bazza. 'And?'

'Baz, this says it's *Night of the Living Dead*.'

'So. What's that difference?'

'What's the difference? It's a completely different film from the one we want. I'd say that's a pretty big difference, wouldn't you?'

'Living dead, evil dead, all the fuckin' same shite to me.'

'Well not to me, Baz.'

'So you don't want it then?'

'No. It's a different film. What aren't you understanding?'

'Cheeky cunt. I'm doing you a favour.'

'Look, the film we want –'

'Oi!' The shout cut across the pub car park. We all turned to see Peroxide and his fat, teardrop-tattooed sidekick come lurching out of the Ghost. I felt my stomach near enough drop out of my arse. Peroxide crossed the car park fast, his eyes fixed on me.

13.

'Fuck you looking at?' said Peroxide, addressing me firmly. I buckled immediately, unable to hold eye contact. I was hoping Paul and Mark would step in, or even Barry; he was an actual adult after all. But no. Not one of them rallied to my defence; they just let me hang.

'Well? Cunt.'

'Nothing,' I muttered.

'You were eyeballing me to fuck.'

'When?'

'Don't get fuckin' cheeky; I'll lace ya. When you came in the pub, you were starin' me out.'

'I wasn't.'

'You fuckin' did. You callin' me a liar?'

'No.'

'So you were staring then?'

'No. I... I didn't.'

Peroxide turned to Teardrop and said, 'Looks like he's gonna shit himself.' They both laughed. Peroxide had broken teeth.

Behind me Bazza shut the backdoors of his van and locked them. He then turned to Peroxide and Teardrop and said, 'Just watch me fuckin' van, alright lads?'

Teardrop said, 'Sure, Baz.'

Then Barry Metcalfe, the master plasterer, walked back to the pub without a backwards glance. We were all too stunned to say anything.

14.

Aside from a few scuffles in junior school, I'd only had one real fight in my life, and that had been with Philip Parkinson when I was in the third year. He had bloodied my nose and cut open my eyebrow, and pretty much the entire school year had watched and cheered. My face had looked a lot worse than it was, but still, there had been no doubt I'd taken a pasting. Yet I seemed to gain some kudos for actually having had the fight in the first place, even if I did lose spectacularly. All I'd done in that bout was flail my arms around wildly and hope something connected with Parkinson's face. Very little actually had. Parkinson, on the other hand, managed to land several punches right on my nose and the blood came pouring out. I never went down though.

That'd all been over fifty pence he'd lent me, which I'd failed to pay back.

I thought of this as I stood in The Silver Ghost car park, wondering how the Parkinson fight had ever felt like such a big deal. Yet it had at the time; it'd played on my mind for weeks afterwards. Every time I saw Philip Parkinson around school I felt sick with nerves. But nothing ever happened again; that'd been the end of it, and before long it was all forgotten.

I even hung out with Philip Parkinson down the park a few times in the fourth year and ended up sitting with him in the school canteen every now and then. Even went round his house once to watch *Hooper* with Burt Reynolds. I had a feeling that such things weren't in store for me and Peroxide. This was going to be bad. Very bad indeed.

15.

It was bad.

16.

Well, bad for Mark anyway. He took the brunt of the assault. I did take a good punch on the jaw from our friend Peroxide at the outset (cutting my lip), but after that the brawl kind of descended into a tangle of grabbing, pulling, hitting, shoving, kicking, spitting and the occasional attempted biting as Peroxide and Teardrop clashed with Mark, Paul and myself; a five man ball of wheeling limbs and obscenities spilling around The Silver Ghost's car park.

I glimpsed some of the pub's patrons standing by the doors shouting and laughing, throwing such encouragements as, 'Go on, lad!' and 'Hit him!' and 'In the face, you clown!' to no one in particular. It's difficult to make much sense of anything while you're in the centre of a brawl, especially when it involves multiple bodies. It was all a bit of a blur. I'm pretty sure I kicked Paul several times by accident, and likewise, I'm sure Mark punched me in the ear (which hurt more than Peroxide's initial whack, I might add). I could hear The Silver Ghost regulars laughing their heads off. I glimpsed the Master Plasterer guffawing with the barman, Alan. There was even a middle-aged woman with a massive perm leant against a Ford Cortina, smoking a fag, watching us with mild amusement.

The fat lad, Teardrop, kicked me in the shins, which killed, and I cried out and tried to kick him back. He didn't seem to like this, and he tried to get me in a headlock, but Paul shoved him away and then grappled him to floor. I assisted Paul by lashing out at the fat kid's every movement. Then, in my peripheral vision, I saw Mark hit the deck, blood spewing from his face.

'And fuckin' stay down, ya cunt,' cried Peroxide, hopping from foot to foot, jacked up on adrenaline.

Mark cupped his nose with both hands, blood spilling between the fingers. Teardrop shoved Paul and I away and got to his feet. 'Fuckin' laced him, Lee,' the fat kid said to Peroxide.

'Fuckin' too right,' replied Lee.

From across the car park, the woman with the massive

perm shouted over, 'Is that it?' and threw her nub-end to the ground and walked back into the Ghost. Alan and Barry both headed back inside as well. The show was over.

'Now get the fuck outta here,' said Lee, to all three of us, 'before I do ya some more damage.'

Mark struggled to his feet, and Paul and I flanked him. And that was that. Peroxide Lee and his fat mate went back into the pub – not before calling us 'puffters' – and we three, scuffed and bloody, headed out into ill-lit streets, our tails between our legs.

17.

'What the hell has happened to you?' said Lindsay on opening the door to us. Mark was still holding his nose; his hands, wrists and chest were covered in blood. Lindsay looked utterly horrified. She took Mark by the arm and guided him through her tiny bedsit, leading him straight into the bathroom.

Paul and I hovered in the doorway. I heard Lindsay run the taps and tell Mark to put his head back. I looked around the room – for it was only *a* room. It was tidy, but so, so small. It was classed as a basement flat; you had to descend a set of steps and walk through a passageway to get to it. The building itself might once have been a grand four storey house, but had long been converted and divided up into cubby-holes for students, doleites, crack-heads and the odd prostitute (Lindsay claimed to have heard *business* being conducted in the flat above her on many occasion). Given the flat's location – at the very bottom and back of the building – and because of its narrow passageway entrance, Lindsay had dubbed her home The Batcave, and so that's what we all called it. I'd only been in the Batcave a few times, once to watch John Carpenter's *Escape from New York*, and once or twice just to call round for Mark (he didn't live there, not officially anyway, but he was there most nights).

The place was indeed poky, but Lindsay seemed to make the most of it. There was a settee and chair in the middle of the room, set before the TV and video, of course; a kitchen area behind that, and off to the side, a bed and all Lindsay's clothes hung on a rail, and that was pretty much it. It was as basic as basic gets, but Lindsay had lived there for near enough a year.

She had left home as soon as she turned sixteen (I don't think she got on with her folks), and, after a few jobs here and there, settled at an insurance company, which she detested; but still, she was self-contained and away from her parents, which was far more than the rest of us could say. I'd heard Mark mention that he and Lindsay were saving up for a bigger place, but that was months ago, and I'd heard nothing more since. She did seem to have it sorted though, did Lindsay. She had her own space – however small – where she could come and go as she pleased, with no one hassling her: no one telling her what time to be in or having to sit at the dinner table at a certain time every night; she could eat when she wanted, go out when she wanted, and watch whatever she liked on the telly. Lindsay worked to pay the rent and all her bills (she had all that stuff sorted), but come Friday, she was out, usually until Sunday. She could drink us all under the table, and often times she'd be the last man standing at the end of the night. She liked Floyd and Kate Bush and AC/DC (she had a poster of Bon Scott on her wall), but she could take or leave Maiden, much to Mark's annoyance. She enjoyed watching horror movies with us, but also liked French films and Woody Allen, which none of us understood. She made her own jewellery, and was always creating something arty and crafty. Lindsay knew exactly who she was, and appeared to be completely comfortable with this knowledge (something which never failed to amaze me). She had just turned eighteen, but seemed far older and wiser than anyone I knew our age.

She came out of the bathroom, shutting the door behind her. Mark was still in there and I could hear the bath running. She looked really pissed.

'So?' she said. She looked from me to Paul, then back to me again.

Paul started. 'It was this twat down the Silver Ghost.'

'What were you doing in there? It's a right dive.'

I cut in. 'Mark knows a bloke who goes in there... he sells videos and we were after this film called *The Evil Dead...*'

She looked at me gone out. 'What?'

I couldn't hold her gaze. 'And there was this lad and he just came up sayin' that I was staring him out...'

'Fuck sake, Scott. This your fault?'

'No, no... I wasn't staring anyone out, promise. You know me...'

'But what you're saying,' she began, 'is that this lad picked a fight with you... so Mark steps in and near enough gets his nose fucking broken?'

'It's not broken is it?' Paul asked, in a kind of awe.

'I'm not sure, Paul, I'm not a nurse. We're gonna have to go down to A&E.... after he's cleaned himself up a bit.'

'I got my lip cut,' I offered, and immediately regretted it.

'Big fucking wow,' she said.

A heavy silence fell on us. I just wanted to get out of there. I could hear Mark splashing water and groaning.

Finally, I said, 'Look, Lindsay... I'm really sorry. I didn't mean for this to happen. I don't go round picking fights with people...'

She seemed to soften a little at this. 'No,' she said. 'No, you don't. You're not a knuckle head; none of you are. Paul thinks he's hard, but we all know he isn't.'

This broke the tension and I laughed. Paul smirked, 'Yeah, yeah, Linz, well you should've seen me tonight – battered this fat kid...'

'That's nothing to be proud of, Paul. Wait a minute, how many of them were there?'

'Two,' I said.

She smiled grimly, 'Two against three, hey? You fucking hardnuts.'

'It wasn't like that, Lindsay,' I said.

She held up her hand. 'I don't care anymore. You've all disappointed me tonight.' Coming from Lindsay, this felt terrible. 'Now, do one, I've gotta get Rocky to the hospital.'

As we were leaving, Mark peered round the bathroom door. He looked like a scolded child. He also looked strange, with the nasty gash across the bridge of his nose, and the snozzle in question at an altogether different angle to its usual place on his face. He'd broken it all right.

'See ya,' he said.

18.

It was getting late, but I didn't much fancy going home so I went back to Paul's house and we threw on David Cronenberg's *Shivers*. We'd picked up some more tinnies from the corner shop and sat side by side on Paul's double bed watching the film. (He was the only lad I knew with a double bed; I was still on the same single bed I'd had since I was about eleven. My feet stuck out the bottom).

We didn't say much for a long while. Paul's bedroom was pretty cavernous, perpetually dark, even in the daytime (he never opened his curtains), with a low ceiling and the walls crowded with posters. He never put the big light on, using only his tiny bedside lamp, which illuminated very little. When the TV wasn't on (which, admittedly, was rare) you really couldn't see shit. The posters were, for the most part, of horror films – a *Dawn of the Dead*, a *Texas Chain Saw*, a *Twins of Evil*, a *House by the Cemetery* – along with one for Maiden's *Killers* album with Eddie stood beneath an ominous night sky on an insipid yellow-lit street, bloody axe in hand, dying hands desperately clawing at the skeletal demon's shirt. There was an awesome one of Susan George in *Straw Dogs* – with some serious nipplage going on – and another of Olivia Hussey in *Black Christmas*. We all loved Olivia Hussey, ever since we were made to watch Zeffirelli's *Romeo and Juliet* back in school and sat awestruck at the sight of her absolutely incredible breasts. They really were spectacular and became the talk of the schoolyard for days, maybe even weeks.

I suppose his room wasn't too dissimilar to my own, only smaller, darker, and smellier (if that was even possible). It wasn't much of a mystery as to why females were a total absence from our lives. However, he did have a video player in his room, which I found just incredible. In fact, it was a source of envy to all who knew him.

Cronenberg's erotic body horror played out before us. Not taking his eyes off the screen, Paul said, 'That Lynn Lowry looks well filthy.'

'She's the one out *The Crazies* ain't she?'

'Yeah. She did loads of soft porn as well.'

'No way!'

'Yeah, man.' He fell silent for a moment, then added, 'Well, she's not exactly shy in this is she?'

I looked at the screen. In the film, a parasite (which, to be honest, looked a bit like a turd) turns the occupants of a high rise apartment block into sex-crazed maniacs. Said parasite was currently inside Lowry's mouth (a turd on a tongue), and she was trying frantically to kiss some bloke and infect him. Her top was tight and, like Susan George on the wall, there was some serious nipplage.

'Those nips are like bullets,' I observed.

'Yup. She's well fit.'

I cracked open another can. 'Fuckin' weird night, man.'

'Shit night ya mean?'

'Well, yeah... I'd fuckin' love to batter that guy.'

'You and whose army?'

'Do one. He wasn't all that. He just got lucky.'

Paul looked at me. 'Mate, you're about as hard as a sandcastle.'

'Witty fucker.'

'No, look...' He took a swig of his can. 'You don't wanna be like them wankers down the Ghost. They're fuckin' D.L.F., man. Utter scum. They've got nothing else in their lives but drinking 'un fighting...'

'And what we got? Drinkin' and watching horror films...'

'Least we appreciate art, man, not some fuckin' overpaid cockend kicking a ball around a field... or more to the point, some fuckin' cockend kicking someone's head in.'

On the screen, Barbara Steele was unknowingly taking a bath with a parasitic turd monster. I knocked back my can. 'I am glad I love all this stuff,' I said. 'It's like... it makes me who I am.'

'Yeah, man,' Paul agreed.

'These films... there's like a weird comfort to them.' Paul looked at me, but I carried on watching the screen. The turd monster had gone up Barbara Steele's snatch and she was writhing around in the bath. I said, 'I just wanna watch horror films for the rest of my life.'

I was pissed, but not so pissed that I didn't know what I was saying. I meant those things, even if I couldn't articulate my feelings very well. At seventeen, horror movies were everything to me, that much was certain, but it occurs to me now they were more than just a distraction from life; they were, in fact, guiding my very existence, shaping my imagination and igniting a passion that would propel me out of Derby, away from the dole queue, and from the prospect of building sites and factories and warehouses. Every time I watched a horror movie I could feel ambition rising in me: an absolute *need* to create growing stronger and stronger with each and every film, no matter how good, bad, or indifferent. In fact, the bad ones sometimes fuelled me more, because I would just think, *I could do loads better than that.* I was convinced that just because I came from a small city in the Midlands didn't mean that I couldn't, or indeed shouldn't, become a filmmaker myself and live a life of dreaming up macabre plots, creating gory effects, and shooting in remote locations with a filmmaking family – just like the guys who made *The Evil Dead* – and have kids like myself all over the world watching the films I created. That was the dream, and with every horror movie, that idea became more and more fixed in my mind.

Naïve this may have been, but at seventeen, this was how I thought. In fact, I felt consumed by the idea. It centred me, and it felt good. Some days my ambition would wane – usually because I'd become bogged down by the pressure of the entire world insisting I get a shit job – and I would find myself feeling lost and depressed. But then I'd throw on a Romero film, or a John Carpenter, and I would be fixed again. I'd think about camera angles while waiting in the job centre and actresses I'd like to cast while my parents continually scolded me about my lack of employment. I'd think up film titles while in job interviews and scribble movie credits on the backs of applications forms: my favourite credit being *written and directed by Scott Bradley.* I could think of nothing else I wanted to do with my life. The only problem was: I had absolutely no idea how to get into the movie business, or more importantly, have the first clue how to even make a film. Still, in the ignorance (arrogance?), and complete naivety of my seventeenth year, I didn't let these minor details get in the way of my daydreams.

I turned to Paul. 'What do you want to do with your life?'

Paul looked horrified. 'Fucking hell, Bradley, you sound like the fuckin' job centre.'

'No... it's just... I know what I want to do; it just seems so out of reach.'

'What?'

'I want to do this,' I said, pointing to the TV.

'What? Become a sex-crazed zombie? I hear ya, buddy.'

'No, I want to make horror films.'

Paul grinned, and in the flicker of the television he looked almost psychopathic. 'Mate, how the fuck are you gonna do that?'

'I don't know. I asked my folks about going to film school.'

'Film school? Where the fuck is that?'

'London.'

'Fuck that, man, it'll cost a bomb. You wanna do it, do it like them *Evil Dead* guys – just get a fuckin' camera and go shoot summat.'

'But what?'

'I don't fuckin' know, you're that one who wants to make a soddin' film.'

We fell silent.

The film was nearing its climax. Lynn Lowry and hordes of other sex-crazed maniacs were dragging the last remaining tower block occupant not infected by the parasite into a swimming pool. Lowry, all wet and wearing a tight top, had more nipplage going on. I said, 'But... don't you wanna do something with your life.'

'I am doing something,' said Paul. 'I'm sitting around drinking and watching horror films. To be honest, that's all I wanna do. I don't want a fuckin' nine to five job draining the life outta me. It's bullshit, man. It's what *they* want you to do... to keep you in line. It's all fuckin' wank. Those millions and millions of sad bastards out there complying, going to work, just to pay fuckin' bills for things they don't even fuckin' need. Me dad walks around like a zombie most of the time; he's fuckin' shell-shocked, man: shell-shocked from a life of going to work day after fuckin' day in that god-awful factory – the same thing every day, over and over. Cunt's nearly sixty now and it's like someone's just turned off the lights in his head. There's nobody there. You try and talk to him and he's just gone. I'm sure the poor cunt is just waiting around to die, just so it'd all be over, y'know?

'Look, I'm sure making films is well wicked, but I'm also pretty sure there's a fuckin' lot of shit that goes with it, man. Plus, it's well hard to get into. If it wasn't, every fucker would be doing it, right?'

'So what you sayin' then?' I said, 'I should just forget about trying to follow my dreams and accept the fact I've just gotta get a shit job and end up turning into a zombie?'

'No, fuck that,' said Paul, cracking open another can. 'Just stay on the dole. There's no fucking jobs out there anyway.'

'Just stay on the dole? What, for the rest of my life?'

'Yeah, fuck it, man. Col Struthers' dad never fuckin' worked a day in his life. How many Struthers are they? Four? Five?'

'Six. They've got an older sister as well.'

'Oh yeah. That guy's got it sorted; he gets the government to pay for his kids and his rent and all that shit and he gets to sits around drinking all day – and shagging, by the sounds of it. He's got a few things on the side as well, I've heard.'

'He sounds like a fuckin' loser,' I said.

'He sounds like he's livin' the fuckin' dream to me. He gets to do want he wants. He hasn't got The Man breathing down his neck, and he gets to drink down the Silver Ghost every fucking day. Sounds great.'

'But don't you want to do more with your life than that?'

'For what? Money? To get a fuckin' mortgage? What's the point in that? You don't really own a house, y'know, it's just an illusion. It's just more bullshit. And if you're loaded they take all your money in tax anyway. Fuckin' George Harrison sang about that, man. I'll be happy just to have enough to do my own thing. Simple as. It's not asking much. Look, you do what you gotta do, Scott, but I'm tellin' ya, it's all wank, man, don't buy into it.'

It was pointless talking to Paul. I watched the end of the film, then drank up and left.

19.

I walked home through quiet streets, wondering how Paul could be so passionate about things – horror films, Iron Maiden, Stephen King novels – and yet only see them as disposable entertainments; something to be enjoyed, but nothing more. Whereas I was positively fuelled by such things; I saw them as art, and they made me want to write, to make, to create. I genuinely couldn't understand why everybody didn't feel the same way. Also, I was troubled by Paul's utter conviction in his own bullshit. He'd always been that way, and beer only emphasised it. Most of what he said was utter drivel, but it was pointless arguing with him when he got in one of those moods. Pointless, because, well, he was really good at arguing, and I'd learnt on many occasions to keep my mouth shut when he got on one of his rambling streams of stupidity. Often there were points he'd make that I would agree with, but the arrogance of his conviction and his penchant for taking a point too far, or, most annoyingly, going off topic all together, would make his original augment moot. Paul lived in a world of his own making and if you didn't agree with that world, he'd go on and on as to why he was right, usually spouting increasingly ridiculous points, but with such utter belief that he simply beat you down.

His parents didn't seem to give him anywhere near as hard a time about getting a job as my mum and dad did me (although they did have their moments), and he hadn't once attempted to look for one since leaving school. I'd been forced to fill out countless application forms and had been on six or seven excruciating interviews, and each time I didn't get the job my dad would grill me as to what I'd said and done in said interview.

The one person that did give Paul shit, and argued with him constantly, was his older brother, Carl. Carl had been the one to introduce Paul to horror films when they were much younger, and they were pretty close for a long time, but after school, Carl went to college and drifted away from home, eventually becoming a police officer, much to the disgust of his younger sibling. Carl had always seemed all right to me, even with the uniform, but every time I'd mention his name, or bring him up in anyway at all, Paul would just go mental. Hence my suggestion about Carl helping us out with the money for *The Evil Dead* being so viciously shot down in flames. Friends were strange beasts.

I turned down my street and groaned as I saw the front room light was still on in our house. I contemplated trying to sneak in the back door, but knew that would be futile: both my parents seemed to possess supersonic hearing. As I approached the house, a breeze kicked up a scattering of leaves and it struck me that the feeling of October is the *feel* of most horror films.

I put the key in the lock and turned it gently. I stepped inside, closing the door as quietly as possible, then turned, and found my dad stood waiting for me in the hallway.

20.

Dad's opening gambit was the immortal classic: 'What time do you call this?'

'Dunno,' I muttered. 'Night time?'

'Don't get cheeky with me, my lad. You're not too old for a clip round the ear.'

I took my jacket off and hung it on the banister. My dad immediately took it off the banister and handed it back to me. 'There's a place for that, Scott, and it isn't there.'

'I know, I just…'

'*I just* nothing, hang it up properly.'

I huffed and went down the hallway and hung my jacket on the decidedly full coat rack beneath the stairs. I had to battle for space. I turned around and my dad was standing right in front of me.

'This isn't on, you know?'

'What?'

'What do you mean *what*? Don't play silly beggars with me, Scott. Your mother was worried; it's gone midnight!'

'I was at Paul's… watching a film.'

'Well you could have called to tell us where you were…'

'I'm not a kid anymore, Dad.'

'Oh, really?' he said, and I just knew by his tone that I'd fallen into a trap. 'Well you could have fooled me, Scott.'

'I'm going to bed,' I muttered, trying to get round him. He pressed a firm hand on my chest and kept me at bay.

'Not so fast, Mister I'm-all-grown-up. Tell me; now you're a man and you think it's all right to come and go as you please in my house and keep your mother up until all hours worrying, have you got any rent money for me? Oh, and what time are you up for work in the morning?

'Oh, wait a minute, that's right, you're not going to work are you… because you're a spoilt, lazy, fucking little gobshite.'

That shook me. His voice was steady, controlled, but the sudden venom with which he said this frightened me so badly I couldn't look him in the eyes; instead I focused on the carpet. I realised that my hands were shaking.

'I want you up early in the morning and ringing about that warehouse job. Got it?'

'Yeah.'

'Pardon?'

'Yes.'

'Good. Better yet, go down there yoursen and fill out the application form there and then. You hear me?'

'Yes.'

'So what are you going to do?'

'Go down there.'

'What? Speak up!'

My eyes were watering and it took everything I had to stop myself from breaking into a full blown cry. I said. 'Go down to the warehouse and fill out the application.' I felt low and pathetic.

'Good. And if I find out you haven't when I get home tomorrow, I swear to God, boy, you will be in for it.'

'I'll do it.' My lips were wobbling.

'Make sure you do. Now go to bed. I'm sick of the sight of you.'

I shot past him and ran up the stairs. Once in my room, I wiped my eyes, fell straight onto the bed and curled up in a ball. I didn't sleep for a long time.

21.

I woke, looked at my clock and saw it was only six. I'd had a restless night and felt groggy and hung-over. The memory of my dad's bollocking returned and I groaned. I rolled over and tried to go back to sleep, but it was futile. I lay there for at least twenty minutes just going over and over all the shit he'd said to me, and remembering the quiet rage with which he had looked at me. I'd very rarely seen my dad mad, like really mad. But the few occasions I'd been witness to it had scared the shit out of me, especially when I was younger. Having his anger directed right at me was devastating, to say the least. In fact, just thinking about it caused my stomach to knot up and my chest to grow tight. He wasn't a dad who would hit me or shout or anything like that, that seemed to be Mum's department, but then he didn't need those weapons in his arsenal; one look across the dinner table could put a stop to any shenanigans in a heartbeat. He'd give me like a Clint Eastwood stare (which I'm pretty sure he modelled on the man himself) and that would be the end of it, whereas mum would rant and rave and I wouldn't take a blind bit of notice. Even a clip round the back of the head – which was a frequent occurrence with Mum – had little to no effect. Dad, however, was in an entirely different league; that man could be scary when he wanted to be.

I needed to take my mind off everything, so I had wank over a girl I'd seen that summer working in Mercury Sounds, our local record shop. She'd modelled her look on Debbie Harry and was really something else. Afterwards I wiped myself down with a t-shirt I swiped from the floor and immediately returned to thinking about the previous night. The entire distraction had lasted no more than three minutes and now I was back worrying about fucking Jobgate and my dad all over again.

Then, as if my mind just wanted to torment me as much as possible, I remembered the fight with Peroxide and Teardrop and Mark's broken nose and the shit Lindsay had given us and Paul's stupid revolt against the system and the fact that I'd told Ray Ellis I'd pay him sixty quid today for a video and

I didn't have it – I didn't even have a fucking pound note to my name, let alone sixty squidlers – and now I had to go down to that sodding warehouse and ask for a job. And to top all that off, I suddenly remembered that I had to go and sign on at eleven.

Fuck.

It'd been a pretty shit night any way you looked at it and today's prospects didn't look any rosier in the slightest. I got up and went to go for a piss.

I gingerly stepped across the landing to the toilet. That was when I heard the flush. My heart settled in my throat. I thought about scurrying back to my bedroom, but it was too late; I heard the lock unlatch and the door opened. The smell hit me before Dad even noticed me standing there. After drying his hands he turned and saw me. 'Ah, boy, glad to see you're up.'

The cheeriness in his tone eased the knot in my stomach a little, but still – 'Mornin'' – was all I could manage.

He stepped out onto the landing, looked back into the toilet and said, 'I'd give that a good airing, son. Come back in twenty minutes.'

I wrinkled my nose and walked back to my room.

'Scott.'

Reluctantly, I stopped and turned, meeting his gaze.

'Remember what I said.' The sternness returned to his voice. 'You get down to that warehouse today, right?'

'I've got to sign on at eleven.'

'And? It's only seven. I want you down the warehouse at nine, on the dot. That'll give you plenty of time to get the application filled in. And it'll give you something positive to tell the dole office.'

He was right about that. It was exhausting coming up with new explanations as to why the breadth of my job search was, let's say, less than impressive. Sometimes, when I couldn't come up with adequate proof I'd done any job hunting, the job centre would threaten to cancel my giro and I'd have to apply for anything going, and attend interviews. That would usually appease them for a few weeks. So telling them I'd been up bright and early applying for a warehouse job would probably buy me at least a month without any further hassle.

I said, 'I'll get washed and dressed, dad, and get over there right away.'

He smiled and looked genuinely pleased – which gave me a pang of guilt – and he said, 'Good lad.' He descended the stairs, offering up this last piece of advice as he went: 'Don't say anything stupid!'

22.

I went back into my room and pulled out a copy of *Fangoria* and stretched out on the bed. I turned to an article on *The Evil Dead*. I looked at the pictures. There was one of Bruce Campbell, playing a character called Ash, shotgun in hand, covered in blood, and another of Sam Raimi, the film's director, and my idol, looking down the lens of his camera. He had a beard, but still looked incredibly young. I wondered what his parents had said to him about pursuing his film-making ambitions. I wondered if they had understood and supported him, or if he'd had to put up with the same kind of shit I had to endure. I reread the article for the umpteenth time and felt it fuel me (at first, anyway). I read about Tom Sullivan, who did the special make-up effects, and imagined myself working with prosthetics and squibs and I wanted it so bad, then I read a section about Raimi, Campbell and Rob Tapert making a short horror film, entitled *Within the Woods*, as a test run for *The Evil Dead*. They'd shot it on Super-8 over six days on a budget of $1,600 (which I worked out to be about £1,000, an astronomical amount of money to me) and used it to encourage investors to back *The Evil Dead*, then called 'Book of the Dead'. The fact that even their short film cost so much depressed me greatly. It occurred to me that I didn't have the first idea about film stock, or camera lenses, shooting schedules, sound recording, editing, mixing, directing actors, or even the first clue as to how to write a fucking screenplay. From the ground up, filmmaking was a complete mystery to me. Who was I kidding?

I threw the copy of *Fangoria* to the floor and lay back on the bed. I felt utterly lost. I turned over and fell asleep in seconds.

23.

I woke up at ten o'clock.

24.

I was three minutes late and missed my allotted time to sign on. Punctuality was a big deal with the job centre and I knew I'd have to make up some excuse or other in order to sign on that dotted line: no signature equalled no dole cheque, and that would be catastrophic.

I told the battleaxe at the inquiry desk that my bus had been late (in fact, I'd had to run to catch it) and that was why I was late. She eyed me with suspicion and huffed in a dramatic manner, then wrote my name down on a piece of paper (she got my name wrong I noticed: *Scot Broadly, 11am*), and told me to join the back of a ridiculously long queue that snaked around the entire job centre. I joined said queue and wanted to die.

25.

Forty minutes later I was greeted with this. 'So... what have you been doing to look for a job?' The question was posed by Jim, an unkempt, plump, middle-aged job centre employee whose soul had long ago been strung up and burned on the funeral pyre of English life, leaving in its wake an empty, doughy torso, with limbs that saw too little movement and a mind that contained nothing but the wreckage of failure and regret.

I answered with my usual monologue, which I had off by heart. 'Well, I've been looking every night in the job section of the *Derby Evening Telegraph* and I've been taking driving lessons in an effort to improve my chances of getting a job. Once I get my licence I can look for jobs further afield; Notts, up in Derbyshire, Leicester even. Also, I regularly go down Assort Drive and go round all the businesses asking if they have any jobs going. I have my name down at loads of companies and they said they'd call me when a position comes up.'

None of that was true.

'And did you find any jobs in the paper?' Jim said, with all the interest of a corpse.

'There's a warehouse job going at Chelful... y'know, down Ashbourne Road, the toy place – I'm applying for that.'

'And these driving lessons,' said Jim, 'how are you paying for them?'

That momentarily stumped me. Jim, who I usually saw when I was signing on, never normally asked anything beyond his usual list of questions. This was a new one, and I wasn't prepared.

'Err,' I began. 'Me dad's teaching me.'

'Oh right, so you're not actually learning to drive with a proper instructor then?'

'No, erm, not yet... but me dad's teachin' me everything he can before I have to start paying for lessons so that I'll be really good behind the wheel already when I start and I won't have to have so many lessons before I can put in for me test.'

'Right.' He didn't seem very convinced. 'And what kind of work are you looking for, Mr Bradley?'

Another new question. This really had never happened before. Jim would usually just ask the initial what-have-you-been-doing-to-look-for-work question and I'd give my rehearsed answer, then he'd hand me the sheet to sign and that would pretty much be that, I'd be outta there. But for whatever reason, Jim had suddenly got curious and I was going have to think fast. Really fast.

I swallowed. 'I'm looking for something where I can be part of a team and work with other committed and enthusiastic people. I know I can work hard and communicate effectively in a team.'

Jim leaned back in his chair, resting his hands on his belly. He looked at me, but didn't say anything. Then he smiled. It was toothy and didn't fit his face at all well. 'Well, that's wonderful to hear Mr Bradley, now if you could just give me an answer that isn't filled with as much bullshit, I'd be most appreciative.'

His teeth were stained and crooked. Something about him made me think of Toad of Toad Hall. I had no idea what to say. Jim stared at me for a moment longer, stretching the silence to an unbearable length, then he said, 'I'll tell you what... you come back in two weeks to sign on and if you haven't got any evidence of extensive job hunting then I will suspend your dole. You understanding me, Mr Bradley?'

I nodded, mouth agape.

'This country isn't a free ride, you know? You have to work and pay your way. It seems I see kids like you every hour of every day – school leavers who think they don't have to raise a finger, freeloading off their parents and the government. You may think Thatcher has sent this country down the swanny, and that may be so, but that doesn't mean you can, or even should, just sit around expecting hand-outs.

'I am going to get you into work, Mr Bradley, if it's the last thing I do. I'm going to give you the grace of two weeks to have a crack at it yourself and if nothing turns up, then you are going to become my very own pet project. Got it?'

I stared at him in stunned silence.

'Well?'

'Yes,' I murmured. 'I understand.'

'Good.' He handed me the booklet to sign. On it was an entire sheet filled with my signature from the weeks and weeks I'd been signing on. I signed and dated it and handed it back.

'Have a good day, Mr Bradley, and remember... your working life starts now. Today. Okay?'

I muttered some kind of agreement and got out of there as fast as possible.

26.

I must have left the job centre looking decidedly shell-shocked. I saw a few other kids with the same stupefied expression staggering from the building. I decided at that moment to walk the two-odd miles from town up Ashbourne Road to the Chelful toy factory and get my name down on an application form. I would have done as well, had it not been for Paul coming bounding up to me saying, 'Bradley, you bellend! You're gonna shit when you see what I got.'

27.

Paul took me round to Duckworth Square, an old shopping precinct that had long since been abandoned. He said he wanted to show me something and didn't want anyone else around. He was being weird.

No one really came down this part of town anymore, save for winos and bockers (bocker was Derby vernacular for a tramp, taken from a notorious pissed up dosser from the sixties named Bocker Wright; my dad had known him, or rather, known of him). All the shops were boarded up, and those that weren't, of course, had all their windows smashed in. Doors hung off hinges (or if not were nailed shut), and newspapers blew about the cracked and weed-ridden paving. There was the odd hypodermic needle and used condom and plastic bags filled with Lord knows what gathered in corners, and also the obligatory overturned shopping trolley and piss-stained chair and matching burnt out settee strewn about here and there.

The precinct had been condemned only a few years before, but the council, in their infinite wisdom, seemed perfectly happy to let it just sit and decay and become a haven for the glitterati of Derby's finest bockers and smack heads. I remembered being brought here by my mother when I was very young, then a thriving part of town, and even recalled her buying me a Matchbox car from a shop that was now spray-painted in big red lettering with the words *Buckle is a twat*.

I turned to Paul. 'Fuck we doin' here?' I said.

He grinned and then riffled through his pockets.

I said, 'Can't believe that prick at the job centre...'

That's as far as I got because Paul handed me a wad of notes.

'Fuckin' bollocks!' I yelled.

He shushed me. 'Am I the fuckin' daddy or what?'

I was dumbfounded. 'But... how?'

'Don't worry about it.'

I started counting. Six crisp ten pound notes and a fiver thrown in for good measure. Sixty five quid all told.

'I can't believe it,' I said. 'Where'd you get it?'

Paul was all smiles. 'Carl.'

'No way!' Carl lent you this?'

'Well he didn't lend it me exactly.'

'What? He gave it you?' I said, astonished. 'That is fucking awesome, man.'

'Yeah, err... he didn't give it me either.'

'Well... what then?'

'I kinda just took it. From his room, like.'

'Shit, man.' Now I was just plain flabbergasted. 'You're kidding?'

'Nope.'

'Mate, he's gonna find out, and when he does, he'll fuckin' batter you.'

'He ain't,' said Paul. 'Cunt hardly ever comes home. He stays at his girlfriend's all the time.'

'But that still doesn't mean he won't find out its gone.'

'Look. Don't worry about it will ya. We've got the money now to get *The Evil Dead*!'

I looked at my friend and wondered if he genuinely believed his brother wouldn't notice the money was missing, or if he just didn't give a shit one way or the other. I knew there was absolutely no love lost between the two, but still, to nick sixty-five quid from your own kin was pretty low, and Carl would indeed tear Paul a new one when he found out. He might even shop him. Judging by how Paul and his dad spoke about Carl and the seriousness with which he took his life in the police force, it wasn't at all out of the realms of possibility. But still, the money would afford us *The Evil Dead* and that in itself was worth the risk.

Something occurred to me. 'You know what?'

'What?' said Paul.

'We get down Ray's, buy the film, then with the rest of the money we'll buy some leads and hook my dad's video player up to yours and we'll make a shit load of copies and sell 'em.'

'Oh, man, like it!'

'If the going rate for *Evil Dead* is sixty-odd quid, we'll only have to sell one, maybe two, and then you can put your brother's money back and he'll be none the wiser. After that, every one we sell is clear profit.'

'You're a fuckin' genius, Scott.'

'I know.'

'We don't have to stop at *Evil Dead* either. We could reel off fuckin' loads of films.'

'Yeah.'

'Yeah, man. Fuck working. We'll just do this. We can pay rent and get the olds off our backs, and still be rolling in it.'

'We'll be raking it in,' I said.

'We won't have a rake big enough, pal.'

We both laughed. The prospect of building a video empire, the likes of which would eclipse Colin, the Pirate Man himself, fixed itself firmly in my mind.

'And you know what?' said Paul.

'What?'

'It was in the paper again this morning... all that video nasty stuff. They're really going to come down hard on all these films, so now's the time to get as many copies as possible, so we can be selling them when they shut down all the video shops.'

'You think they're really gonna shut down every video shop?'

'That's what they're sayin'. They're fucking mental, man. It's like a witch hunt. Turn on the news or read a paper for once, man, and you'll see. There's all these inbred politicians and this dotty old woman ranting and raving about how evil these films are and how they're depraving children 'un all that shit. It's fucking hilarious.'

'What they gonna do?'

'Dunno, but someone's listenin' because there seems to be more and more raids on video shops and more and more people being arrested for owning horror films. It is actually mental. These films are gonna be well hard to get hold of, I'm tellin' ya, and if we've got loads of copies...'

'We'll make a killing.'

'Bingo.'

We fell silent, stunned by our own genius. An old bloke, who looked like he hadn't washed since the year dot, came shuffling around the precinct, riffling around in some plastic bags. Paul noticed him and shouted, 'Oi! You bocker!' and we both laughed and ran towards the street. I heard the tramp shout, 'Wankers!' and that only made it funnier.

28.

Around the corner from the derelict precinct we stopped running and caught our breath. I said, 'Let's get to Ray's then and buy us *The Evil Dead*.'

'We gotta call round for Mark first.'

'He not at work?'

'No, you dipshit, he broke his nose. Spoke to him on the phone this morning. He was at the Infirmary all night. Apparently, he's got two black eyes. Bet he looks like a fuckin' panda.'

I laughed. 'Oh, right,' I said. 'You mean we got to go all the way to Allenton to pick him up, why can't he just meet us there?'

'He's not at home. He's still at Lindsay's. Stayed the night. Bet he was splurting all over it.'

'*It?*'

'Lindsay. You can just tell she fuckin' loves it.'

The Batcave was just across town, so we began walking, and Paul continued to speculate on Lindsay's sexual proclivities, surmising that she had a penchant for anal. He talked for a full ten minutes or more on the subject and had clearly given the matter a lot of thought. I found myself getting more and more annoyed listening to him and tried several times to change the subject, but Paul wouldn't have it. He just wanted to rattle on, in great detail, about all the things he believed Lindsay was well up for.

By the time we reached the Batcave he'd convinced himself that Lindsay was 'gagging' to have all three of us 'gang bang' her, but because she knew Mark would go mental at the merest suggestion she keeps the fantasy to herself and instead just 'flicks her bean' thinking about it every night. Then he went on to describe all the positions we could 'do her in' during said gang bang and how much she'd love it. I wanted to smack him in the mouth. Mercifully, we reached the Batcave and as we walked down the passageway he finally shut the fuck up.

Lindsay answered the door and Paul nudged me and sniggered. I ignored him, as did Lindsay, although I'm not entirely sure she even noticed. She invited us in and we found Mark sitting on the settee looking very sorry for himself. He had a large bandage right across the lower half of his face, above which peered two awful looking purple, swollen eyes. He looked a real mess.

'Alright, panda,' said Paul.

'Do one,' said Mark and carried on watching the TV. They had *Blue Collar* on with Richard Pryor and Harvey Keitel. The tracking was shit and the picture kept jumping. It was most probably a pirate.

Paul sat down next to Mark. 'What's this?'

Mark told him and then got up and paused the video. Lindsay put the kettle on.

I sat down in the chair across from Mark and Paul. 'How you feeling?' I said.

'Shit,' Mark returned. 'We were down the Derby Infirmary until fuckin' four in the morning. I'm knackered.'

'I bet,' I said.

From the kitchen behind me, Lindsay said. 'Who wants tea?'

We all put up our hands and I heard Lindsay clatter about getting mugs out of the cupboard.

Paul said, 'Got a day off though, mate. All good.'

'All good?' said Mark. 'You really are clueless, ain't ya? I don't go in, I don't get paid, pal. I'll be havin' the rest of the week off, which is gonna fuck my money right up.'

'Don't you get sick pay?' Paul looked genuinely confused.

'No. I work cash in hand. No sick pay, no holidays, nothing. If I don't go in I get jack shit.'

'Oh, right,' was all Paul offered further on the subject.

Lindsay poured the water into a teapot and then came around the side of my chair and bent over and turned the TV and video off. I glanced at Paul and saw he was looking at me with a sly smirk on his mush. I looked at my shoes until Lindsay went back to the kitchen.

'Tea's just mashin'' she said. 'Scott, I always forget, do you have two sugars or just the one?'

'One please.'

'K,' she said.

'Paul, you're no sugars, aren't you?'

'Yeah. Cheers.'

'Anyway,' said Mark, 'what you wastrels been up too?'

'I've just been to sign on,' I said.

'Yeah, I've got to go next week,' said Paul. 'It's a right ballache.'

Mark said, 'My heart bleeds.'

'Think they're having some kind of push on getting people into work,' I said. 'Guy there gave me a right hard time about getting a job.'

'Good,' Mark said, and it made me angry.

'He said he was gonna stop my dole if I didn't show I'd been looking for work.'

'Just say you've been looking in the paper and that you've got some interviews lined up,' said Paul. 'That's all I do.'

'That's what I do too, but he wasn't buying it today.'

'What a wanker,' said Mark, as sarcastic as you like.

Lindsay handed me my tea. I said thank you and then she passed Mark and Paul their mugs. Seating being limited, I stood up and offered her the chair, but she waved away my gesture and sat on the floor by the telly. She curled her legs up beneath her, and I found something graceful and utterly feminine in the action.

'Anyway,' said Paul. 'Me and Scott have got a plan that'll sort us out for money.'

I suddenly felt that I didn't want Lindsay to hear about our pirate video empire; that it would lower her already low estimation of us. To be honest, I wasn't sure what her estimation of me was, but I was aware that she spoke to me differently than she did to Paul, for who she would often have outright disdain.

She displayed this at that very moment, saying to him, 'Oh, I can't wait to hear this,' and I knew she would shoot our plan down in flames. There was no stopping Paul though; he had a clear vision for the empire and he wasn't going to let any disapproval from anyone, especially Lindsay, stop him now.

So Paul reeled off the masterplan with no contribution from me. He told them about the money and how and where he'd got it. Mark and Lindsay both pulled him up on this, but just like he'd been with me, he didn't seem to care. He told them about making copies of *The Evil Dead* and other such titles, and again spoke about how these films were going to become highly sought after once the authorities pulled them all off the market. For the most part, Mark remained quiet, but Lindsay challenged him on almost every aspect of the scheme, until I could see that Paul was becoming increasingly irritated. Finally he cracked. 'Well, you're not part of it anyway, Lindsay, so you don't have to worry about it, do you?'

'Fine with me,' said Lindsay. 'I'll just come and watch when you're up in court.'

Mark didn't say a word.

29.

The four of us left the Batcave. Paul led the way, armed with fixed scowl and sixty-five quid burning a hole in his pocket. I trailed behind, my thoughts tangled in a knot of jobs, my dad, the dole office, and a pirate video empire that Lindsay had completely ruined for me. I was surprised that Lindsay had even tagged along, but I guessed she just wanted to keep an eye on Mark (and make sure we didn't get him into any more trouble).

We walked back through town towards Ray's Video Emporium, none of us saying much of anything. The day was overcast and distinctly autumnal. Red leaves scattered along the pavements in bustles and there was a gentle nip in the breeze. Pumpkins leered out from shop windows and one or two storefronts displayed white-sheet ghosts and the odd overgrown spider, complete with plastic web. There was a selection of witches hats and goblin masks in Woolworth's window, along with a sexy looking red devil outfit. I immediately imagined Lindsay in it.

We cut through the Eagle Centre, which was packed with shoppers; mainly mothers with pushchairs, old people, and the occasional young doleite like ourselves; took a right at Marks & Sparks and slipped out the other end. We passed Mercury Sounds: The Cure blasting from within, 'A Forest' to be exact, and then went down through the underpass. A scruffy busker was fumbling through 'The Times They Are A-Changin''. He mumbled the parts he didn't know, and his voice and his slightly out of tune guitar echoed around the tunnel as the relentless noise of cars rumbled overhead. Lindsay dropped ten pence into the open guitar case by his feet and the busker gave her a nod and carried on murdering Dylan.

Once we were through the underpass, Paul said, 'Just gonna nip in the Paki shop – fuckin' starving.'

So we went into Sangra's Convenience Store and Paul sated his appetite with two bags of Monster Munch and some Opal Fruits, which he didn't share. I bought a bag of pickled onion Space Raiders, which I devoured in seconds. Mark and Lindsay didn't get anything.

On my way out I noticed the papers. One of which was *The Daily Mail*. The cover read: BAN VIDEO SADISM NOW. I wondered how long this media and political panic had been going on, or more to the point, how long I'd been oblivious of it. I thought about showing the others, but decided against it and walked on out the shop.

We walked along London Road, past the Derby Royal Infirmary, where Mark and Lindsay had spent most of the night, and left the town centre behind us and headed for Alvaston, the district where Paul and I lived, and where Ray's Video Emporium lay.

At one point Mark stopped and pulled out a bottle of something from his jacket.

'What's that?' I asked.

'Painkillers,' he said, and swallowed two down in quick succession without any water. I could not have done that. 'Have to take 'em every four hours or summat. And I can't drink.'

Paul chimed in. 'You can't drink?'

'Nah. It's a fuckin' pisser, man. If I see that albino cunt again…'

'You'll what?' said Lindsay.

'He wasn't an albino,' I said.

'Nothing, babe.'

'… He just had his hair dyed well gay.' No one was listening to me.

'No, come on,' said Lindsay, 'You'll what… try and lace him?'

'Maybe,' said Mark.

Lindsay sighed. 'Mark, if anyone so much as breathes on that nose, you'll be in agony.'

Paul said, 'We'll batter him for you, mate.'

Lindsay snapped, 'What? Like you did last night?'

A fair bit of colour touched Paul's cheeks. 'Yeah, well, we had to contend with that other lad – there was some right tonnage on him. Me and Scott could drop that lanky streak of piss if he was on his own.'

I wasn't so sure about that. Lindsay said, 'Ooh, you hard nut. Two against one. You big man.'

Paul didn't like that. I could see he wanted to say something back, but he glanced at Mark and decided against it. Instead, he shrugged his shoulders, attempting to show he didn't care what Lindsay had to say, and carried on down London Road. None of us said anything until we passed Dead Man's Lane and Mark looked at the street sign and said, 'Wonder why it's called that?'

'It was a plague pit,' said Lindsay.

'A what?' said Paul.

'It's where they put all the dead bodies during the great plague. The bones of piles and piles of victims of the black death lie under our feet.'

We were all suitably impressed.

Paul said, 'That is well wicked.'

'Yeah,' I agreed.

Mark said, 'When was the great plague and all that?'

'About the fourteenth century, I think...' said Lindsay. 'Or thereabouts.'

We carried on past Wilmorton College and into Alvaston, still talking about the plague. Lindsay knew a surprising amount of medieval history and it helped alleviate some of the tension. Lindsay explained how people's skin would turn black from bubonic plague and their groin would enlarge (to which Paul said, 'Wicked') and ooze pus and smell rotten, and black lesions would pock-mark the body, and noses and ears and fingers, and yes, even dicks, would fall off as the body began to decompose even while the victim was still alive. She told us that great scores of people would be cast into these plague pits while they were still conscious, if not exactly functioning, and would lie amongst the unimaginable stench and decay of their fellow villagers or town folk, and in many cases, their own family and friends, as they too slowly succumbed to the totality of the Black Death.

As we entered the video shop, Lindsay was telling us about sinister sounding plague doctors who wore masks fashioned with half a foot long noses, curved like some grotesque beak (filled with strong smelling substances to counteract the stench of death), with eerie looking gasmask-like eye holes, dark wide-brim hats and coal-black robes, who walked with a cane, used to shoo or, most probably, beat away the infected, and Paul was saying, 'I want to dress up as one for

Halloween,' and Ray was boxing up videos, and the radio was on, and suddenly, and very completely, I had an idea for a film.

30.

Ray had on Radio One, crackling from a tinny old transistor behind the counter. It was *Steve Wright in the Afternoon* and the D.J. himself was telling the nation that they had just heard the country's number one record, 'Karma Chameleon' by Culture Club (Boy George had confused Paul mightily when first he'd seen him), and Ray appeared to be clearing the shop of videos. Mark said, 'Hey, Ray, what's happening?'

Ray turned around, looking stricken. His hair was wild and his skin dark beneath the eyes. He was smoking a fag and spoke with it hanging out the side of his gob. He said, 'Gotta pack up all the horrors.'

'Why?' I said.

'Had a tip off.'

He grabbed *The Gestapo's Last Orgy* and *The Witch Who Came from the Sea* from off the shelf and slotted them a cardboard box filled with other such disreputable titles.

'A tip off?' I said.

'Looks like I'm gonna be raided,' said Ray, sealing the box with masking tape. He stumped his fag out in the ashtray on the counter and immediately lit another. 'Karma Chameleon' gave way to 'Is There Something I Should Know' by Duran Duran and it kept losing the frequency; Simon Le Bon washed out by hiss.

'Raided? said Paul. 'By the police?'

'Yeah. Mate of mine who owns a shop in Chesterfield rang me this morning. He was raided yesterday – they took all his stock and the poor bugger might be prosecuted. Said that the Derbyshire Constabulary are on the warpath. Said I needed to get anything incriminating out the shop.'

'Fuckin' hell, Ray,' said Mark. 'Anythin' incriminating? You'll have nothin' left!'

'Tell me about it,' said Ray, a fag in one hand and *Eaten Alive* in the other.

I realised that now probably wasn't the best time to inquire about *The Evil Dead* and instead asked Ray if he had a pen and paper. He eyed me a little suspiciously, then lent over the counter and handed me a notebook and a pencil. I thanked him and took to the windowsill to scribble down my film idea.

Lindsay came over and said, 'What ya doin'?'

I wanted to tell her that all her plague talk had inspired an idea for a story, but I kept it to myself and instead said, 'Oh, I just need to make a note of something I gotta do.'

She seemed to accept this and went back over to Mark, leaving me to write. Ray continued to pack away certain titles from his stock while Mark, Lindsay and Paul stood about looking decidedly at a loose end. Once Ray had three full boxes of tapes, he enlisted Mark and Paul to help him carry them out back. I continued to write and Lindsay scanned the now threadbare shelves, picking up a video box here and there. I saw her looking at Dennis Hopper's *Out of the Blue* as Men At Work's 'Down Under' came on the radio. Then I heard Lindsay said, 'Fuck.'

I looked up and saw her peering through the glass of the shop door.

'What?' I said.

Without looking at me, she said, 'Two police cars have just pulled up outside.'

31.

I abandoned what I was writing mid-sentence, folded the paper up and put it in my jeans pocket. I could hear voices returning through the back of the shop; it was primarily Paul's voice I caught, but couldn't really make out what he was saying. Lindsay was backing away from the door and I stood up and saw three uniformed police officers and one bloke in a pale suit walking toward the shop. The fella not in uniform looked like he'd stepped right out of *The Sweeney*; loose tie, ill-fitting suit, boot-leather face: walking cliché. Paul and Mark came back into the shop via the door behind the counter and they saw what was happening immediately. I heard Mark say, 'Oh, no', then Ray finally came in just as Lindsay said, 'Fuck, Ray, they're here!' alerting him to the shitstorm about to go down.

The Jack Regan wannabe was first through the door, his underlings following suit, piling into the shop and surrounding us in seconds. They blocked both exits. Then Paul said, 'Carl?' and I could hear panic in his voice, and I looked over and Paul's older brother was stood leering at us from beneath the tit on his head. Then I noticed something that made my heart sink even further into my bowels: in Paul's hand was a VHS copy of *The Evil Dead*.

32.

'Mr Raymond Ellis?' It was the Regan wannabe, his voice about as pleasant as sandpaper across a blackboard: another cliché. He stared at Ray, and only Ray.

The Emporium's proprietor stood rigid in his usual spot behind the counter, eyes like bowling balls. He answered 'Yes' in a decidedly shaky voice and took to occupying himself with lighting another cigarette.

'Mr Ellis, my name is Detective Inspector Bill Moir. I'm leading a special unit to seize and destroy all obscene material from video outlets in the East Midlands. I have all the necessary paperwork here in order to search the entirety of your premises and seize any stock which I deem... unsavoury.'

'But...' began Ray, his voice somewhat steadier, 'what you might deem as unsavoury, I might see as perfectly acceptable–'

'I don't doubt it, but with all due respect, Mr Ellis, your personal taste is irrelevant in this argument. I have a list of seventy-two films that directly violate the Obscene Publications Act of 1959. The Director of Public Prosecutions personally drew up the list with the aid of the National Viewers' and Listeners' Association in order to assist local authorities up and down the country to identify these depraved films. And after viewing many of these titles myself, I can testify that they are indeed depraved. Made by maniacs and serial killers.'

Ray stifled a laugh, and said, 'You think horror films are made by actual psychopaths?'

'They must be!' said Moir. 'Only a person of unspeakable depravity could come up with such loathsome pictures. I saw that Chainsaw video – only a maniac could make such a true depiction of evil.'

Ray grinned and blew smoke through his nostrils, but said nothing further. Everyone was rigid with anticipation, even Moir. It felt like a scene from a Sergio Leone western – the stillness before the gunfire.

Carl was stood, like a coiled spring, directly behind his little brother, and had an extremely unpleasant smile plastered on his mush. Detective Inspector Bill Moir leant on the counter and turned his attention to us. The last thing I wanted.

'And who might you be?' he said, referring to us all.

Not one of us said anything.

Moir smiled and said, 'Very quiet and well behaved aren't they, P.C. Mansell.'

Carl answered, 'Yes, sir. Apart from…'

'Apart from what?'

'Apart from the fact they seem to be in possession of an obscene video cassette, sir.' Paul and I looked at one another in total disbelief.

'Really?' said Moir, sounding genuinely excited.

'Yes, sir.' Carl motioned to the video in his brother's hand. 'That one.'

I clocked Ray wince. Moir was over to Paul in a flash and grabbed him by the wrist, pulling the box up to his eye line. '*The Evil Dead*,' Moir read aloud. '"The most ferociously original horror film of the year" – Stephen King. He's another sicko.'

'Yes, sir,' said Carl.

I stood dumbfounded. I knew for a fact that Carl had read everything Stephen King had ever written and was instrumental in turning Paul onto King as well. I just couldn't comprehend what was happening.

'Hand it over, son,' Moir said to Paul, and Paul did so, although I could see it pained him beyond measure. Moir went back to the counter and placed the video box in front of Ray. Paul looked like he wanted to tear Carl a new one.

'Know anything about this… *film*, Mr Ellis?'

'Not a sausage. Must be the kid's.'

Paul snapped his head round at Ray, but Ray avoided his eye.

'So he didn't hire this film from you?' Moir pressed.

'No, Detective Inspector,' said Ray.

Moir turned back to Paul. 'How old are you, kid?'

Paul licked his lips. 'Seventeen.'

'Did you hire this video from this establishment?'

Paul again glanced at Ray, but got nothing, so he looked around at us.

Moir said, 'You don't need your friends to help you, or Mr

Ellis, for that matter. Now. Did you hire this diabolical excuse for a film from this establishment?'

Paul remained silent. He looked terrified.

His brother nudged him. 'Speak when you're spoken to.'

That was the moment I really began to detest Carl.

'Well?' said Moir.

Paul panicked and blurted, 'I bought it.'

I heard Ray sigh, but I didn't look at him; I couldn't take my eyes off Paul.

'You bought it,' said Moir. 'From here?'

Another trap. I could see sweat breaking out on Paul's forehead. His eyes were massive.

'What is your name, boy?'

This Paul could answer. 'Paul Mansell, sir.'

'Mansell,' repeated Moir. He looked at his P.C., stood directly behind Paul.

Carl appeared reluctant to speak, but said, 'He's my brother, sir,' unable to hide his disappointment.

Moir yelled, 'My goodness! I see the family resemblance now!'

Paul said, 'I look nothing like that cockend.'

I saw Carl's smile loosen a little at that.

Moir said, 'This isn't going to affect your duty, is it, police constable?'

'No, Detective Inspector, not in the slightest.'

I wanted to kick in him right in the cunt.

'Well, it is a small world, isn't it?' said Moir.

'Yes, sir,' said Carl.

Suddenly, Lindsay cut in and said, 'Jesus, Carl, could you get your tongue any further up the Inspector's arse or what?'

Carl went red and looked at Lindsay in a manner that suggested he wanted to beat her repeatedly with his truncheon. Moir, however, laughed his head off. Even the other two police officers sniggered, although they both suppressed it well. Ray's expression remained grim, as did Mark's, but Moir laughed so hard and loud that it was kind of infectious. Before long both Paul and I were giggling. Lindsay remained completely deadpan, eyes fixed on Carl, which only made it funnier. It was a surreal moment.

Finally, Moir regained some control, wiped his eyes with the back of his hand, and said to Lindsay, 'Well, my dear, you've certainly got P.C. Mansell pegged.' – Carl looked devastated – 'What's your name?'

'Lindsay Strutton.'

'Well, Miss Strutton, as amusing, and quite possibly true, as your little quip was, if you insult one of my officers again I shall have you arrested for harassment.'

Me and Paul stopped laughing. Moir said this through a smile, his voice as friendly as could be. It was creepy.

Lindsay looked astonished. I could see she wanted to say something, but remained quiet. Carl leered.

'Now, where were we?' said Moir.

No one answered him.

'Oh yes,' he said. 'Righto men, turn this place over.'

He really did think he was in *The Sweeney*.

Carl shoved his brother back against some the shelves, video boxes falling to the floor. The other two officers – one a black lad I'm sure I recognised – pushed past me and Lindsay. Mark remained fixed to the wall, watching the scene unfold before him, not saying a word.

Carl and the other officers then rushed passed Ray, almost knocking him over, and began to pull videotapes from behind the counter.

'You can't do this!' cried Ray, but Moir just smiled.

Paul caught my attention. He cocked his head towards the door. I gave a slight nod. I looked at Mark and Lindsay and saw that they too were on board with our unspoken plan.

I wasn't sure whether to just make a run for it, or try the more subtle tactic of slowly shuffling nearer to the door and then making a bolt for it when Moir's back was turned. I looked over at the others and they appeared to be in the same quandary.

That was when I noticed Moir clock our little exchange of glances and I knew instantly it was our undoing. He smiled that horrible weasel smile of his and, without a word, strode past us to the door. I closed my eyes as I heard the deadlock drop.

33.

Throughout all this, the radio was still playing, yet I'd hardly noticed it since the arrival of Moir and his lickspittles. I focused in on the sound as I watched the police constables pull apart Ray's video shop. Our video shop.

David Bowie's 'China Girl' was playing and there was something in Bowie's vulnerable, yearning delivery that really affected me. When I'd first heard the Bowie remake of the song he originally wrote and recorded with Iggy Pop in 1977, I'd hated it – that slick Nile Rogers production; radio friendly vomit – and much preferred Pop's raw and emotional version from *The Idiot*. But in that moment, as I watched Carl and the other police officers seemingly tear my entire world down, the pull of that song – Bowie's voice, Stevie Ray Vaughan's guitar – all made for an extremely powerful moment. It may seem like a simple thing, but it is something I'll never forget.

Then the song ended and Billy Joel's 'Uptown Girl' came on and the moment was destroyed.

The coppers were piling tapes and Moir watched with that smile of his, the corners of his mouth twitching. No one was saying anything and the tension was unbearable; Joel's horrible doo-wop throwback not making things any better. The entire situation seemed kind of unreal. Ridiculous even.

I looked at *The Evil Dead* video box which still sat on the counter. I wondered if Paul had already paid Ray the sixty quid. The cover was wonderful, coloured in vibrant purples, greens and reds. It wasn't like other video covers; the artwork had a kind of homemade quality to it, but was striking nevertheless. It put me in mind of the old E.C. Comics from the fifties, which I'd seen in horror books and magazines. The Stephen King quote dominated one half of the picture, and a vivid green witch (or Candarian demon?), hands outstretched, appeared to lunge towards us. She looked awesome. Below this was a skull and in bold red lettering, THE EVIL DEAD. I saw the logo for Palace Pictures in the right hand corner. It was quite a cover.

Never before had I wanted to see a film so badly. Before or since. And it was just sitting there, on Ray's counter, more than likely already our property (well, technically Paul's – no, scratch that, Carl's, ha!), if money had indeed changed hands, and these fuckers were going to snatch it away from us. And for what? I couldn't get me head round it.

Confused, angry, and unable to take the tension (and Billy Joel) anymore, I spoke up. 'This is insane,' I began.

Everyone looked round at me – Moir still grinning.

'They're just films. How can you say what we can and can't watch? They're not going to corrupt me. A horror film isn't going to turn me into a homicidal maniac any more than watching *Smokey and the Bandit* is going to make me want to bootleg booze and drive really fast.

'How can you even suggest that the average person cannot decide for themselves what they want to watch? If you don't like something, just turn it off! It's that fucking simple. We don't need policing. This is ridiculous!'

I ran out of steam and fell silent. Everyone just stared at me. I knew I hadn't given the most cohesive argument in history and felt incredibly frustrated that I couldn't fully articulate my feelings. 'Uptown Girl' finally ended and Steve Wright gleefully introduced Kajagoogoo's 'Too Shy' and I wanted to die.

Moir said, 'Well. That was about the stupidest series of words I think I've ever had the misfortune to hear.' He said this in his overly polite tone, again wearing his trademark smile. There really was something not right about the guy.

Then Lindsay said, 'No! He's right!' Referring to me.

Moir said, 'I beg your pardon?'

'This is nothing but a ridiculous moral panic spearheaded by evangelical backbenchers and one dotty old woman and whipped up into a frenzy by right-wing tabloids who have absolutely no grip on reality.'

That was what I meant to say.

'This is a massive deception and you're all being played.' She pointed at Moir. His smile was slipping. 'All that's happening here is a small number of simple-minded people, with a bit of power, trying to stake their claim on history. They don't like something, so they think no one else can or should enjoy it. There are no critical voices being heard in this shambles. It's nothing but a witch hunt. It's like something out of George Orwell.'

Moir gave Lindsay a slow clap. I could see her seething.

'Rousing stuff, Miss Strutton, but nonsense nevertheless,' he said. 'These films *are* of grave public concern – they are sick, plain and simple, and this media frenzy, as you put it, is entirely justified. These video players are in houses where children have easy access to them. What do you think happens to a child's mind when it sees films filled with sex, depravity and brutal and bloody murder? It is our obligation to the young and vulnerable of this country to protect them from images created by madmen. And not only that, Miss Strutton, they are in breach of the law of this land, and parliament and individuals like Mrs Whitehouse will bring this to its rightful conclusion: a total ban of obscene material, and put peddlers like Mr Ellis here completely out of business. Or even better, behind bars.'

'Go to prison?' said Lindsay. 'For hiring out films he had no part in making?'

'He is a peddler, Miss Strutton, feeding young minds, such as yourselves, with visions of unspeakable wickedness and depravity.'

Lindsay laughed. Actually laughed in Moir's face. His smile twitched like mad.

Suddenly, Mark spoke, which was a surprise to us all. 'What kinds of films do you like, Detective Inspector?'

Moir looked at him. 'Bloody hell, son, what happened to you?'

'I broke my nose.'

'Oh dear,' he said, his grin widening again. 'I don't have time to sit around watching films.'

'But you must watch the occasional film?' said Mark.

'I like Westerns,' he confessed.

'Good stuff. So do I. I love watching the glorified violence – all that mythologizing of actual thieves and murders, and the celebration of a country that butchered its indigenous population in order to steal land and gain absolute power by way of the gun. Wholesome stuff, Inspector.'

Moir's smile positively spasmed.

34.

After that, things really went south. The young black officer began snooping around the backroom, while Carl and the other officer, a lanky, dopy-looking bloke in his mid-thirties, stayed in the shop, sorting through tape after tape. Ray chain-smoked; his eyes darting about wildly, his defiant grin exposing fag-stained teeth. But I could see the bitter cracks in that smile. He was shitting himself: I knew it, my mates knew it, but most of all, Moir knew it, and his own creepy, Joker-like rictus grew increasingly demonic. It had become a place of weird smiles.

I could hear the P.C. out back, clattering and banging about. Then it all went quiet and I saw Ray put both hands to his face and drag his fingers down the skin, pulling at his eyelids. His pupils were bloodshot. He knew what was coming.

The black officer returned and said to Moir, 'You should see this, sir. I've found three boxes of video nasties in the boot of a Capri Ghia out in the jitty.'

I don't think I'll ever forget that line.

The P.C. continued, 'The vehicle was unlocked, sir, and I took the liberty of performing a brief inspection of the tapes. I recognised most of the titles from the Obscene Publications list, sir.'

I looked over at Moir, fully expecting his smile to have become even more ludicrous, but instead his face was stern and quite unnerving. He looked at Ray, but Ray wouldn't, or couldn't, hold his gaze.

'Good work, P.C. Benton,' said Moir, his eyes still fixed on Ray. 'Take Mansell and Spong –' Paul and I let out a giggle at that; the lanky P.C. looked deeply offended; Moir shot us the dirtiest look you could imagine. '– and bring me these boxes of videos.'

'Yes, sir,' said P.C. Benton. He moved to go, but then P.C. Spong said, 'Detective Inspector, I think I've found something down here as well!'

Spong was bent over, rummaging beneath the counter. I knew what lay down there. We all did. Spong came back up, a tape in each hand.

'What are they, P.C. Spong?' enquired Moir.

Spong looked at the titles, sticky labels scrawled in Ray's almost illegible hand. 'I believe they are of a pornographic nature, sir.'

'Really?' said Moir, his smile returning. 'What makes you say that, Spong?'

Paul sniggered.

Spong held one of the tapes up in Moir's general direction and said, 'Because, sir, this one's called *The Erotic Adventures of Dickman and Throbbin.*'

35.

So Ray Ellis of Ray's Video Emporium, the centre of our entire world, was arrested, and I watched in stunned silence as he was handcuffed and read his rights. Everything felt utterly surreal. P.C. Benton had the honour of making the actual arrest, and I noticed that Carl was clearly sulking as he looked on – full pout, bottom lip out and everything – presumably because he had no part of this particular glory. He had, after all, failed to turn up a single incriminating video, aside, that was, from pointing out *The Evil Dead*. Benton and Spong, however – particularly Benton – had hit the mother lodes, and Moir was gushing with pride at his two star pupils. P.C. Mansell was out the picture, given the lowly task of cataloguing each tape. He looked really pissed.

P.C. Spong turned off the radio (cutting off Michael Jackson's 'Thriller') and assisted Carl. I watched as the lanky twat swiped the copy of *Evil Dead* from the counter and shoved it into one of the boxes. That snapped me from my daze and I blurted out, 'That's ours!' Everyone looked at me. Spong saw I was addressing him.

'What is?'

'The film you've just put in that box – *Evil Dead* – it's ours.'

It was a last ditch effort.

From behind me, Moir said, 'And I'll ask again. Where did you get it?'

That did me. I glanced at Ray, now handcuffed, eyes wide, P.C. Benton stood at his side, then at Paul, but he had nothing but a dumb expression carved on his phizog. I said, 'Doesn't matter. That's our video and you have no right to take it.'

It was the best I could do.

'Listen, kid,' said Moir. 'I have every right to take it. It is an obscene film and is, therefore, illegal. Now I strongly suggest you drop this, otherwise I might nick you for possessing obscene material as well.'

'But...'

'Drop it, kid.'

Then something happened that still amazes me to this day. Paul rushed over and pushed P.C. Spong hard in the chest. The officer flew back, his gangly arms flailing about in the air, and smashed straight into Carl. They both went over.

All hell broke loose.

Paul made a grab for *The Evil Dead* and had it within his grasp when P.C. Benton pretty much rugby tackled him to the ground. Paul let out a yell. Then Mark stepped in and tried to wrestle Benton off of Paul. Lindsay screamed for them to stop, but the three of them writhed around on the floor in an absurd tangle of arms and legs. Then Carl and Spong were up and on them and it became an absolute pile on. I looked at Moir, who was actually laughing, hard, but with Lindsay shouting and screaming it hardy registered. I had no idea what to do.

Carl had his brother in a headlock and Paul's face had gone an impressive shade of red. Benton and Spong had Mark pinned down, his face eating carpet, his bandaged nose bloody again. As much as he struggled to escape their hold, it was futile. I stepped forward – I didn't know whether I was going to help Mark and Paul or what – but Lindsay grabbed my coat and pulled me back. I looked round at her and she just shook her head.

Then Ray spoke up, his eyes on Mark and Paul, and simply said, 'You dumb twats.'

36.

Mark Jones and Paul Mansell were arrested at 3:35pm on the 27th of October, 1983. They were driven off in the same squad car as Ray Ellis.

Carl did the driving.

37.

Lindsay and I stood on the pavement outside Ray's. We watched the two police cars roll on down the road. Carl in front, our friends in handcuffs in the backseat, and Moir and the other officers in the rear car, loaded up with Ray's videos, including our copy of *The Evil Dead*.

The sun was sinking, and the street was aglow with a beautiful shimmering haze. I knew from books I'd read that filmmakers referred to this gloaming as the *magic hour*, and it certainly was. The breeze kicked up and leaves scattered along the pavement. There was the sound of kids playing from a nearby park. The police cars turned a corner and were gone from sight and I had a profound moment of clarity: if I didn't make something of myself and get out of this place, I was going to die in this town.

I looked at the video shop, all dark and empty. At that moment, it felt like the end of everything. I turned to Lindsay. Her eyes glistened in the orange haze. Mark really was a lucky bastard. She looked at me, wiped her eyes with the backs of her hands, sniffed, and said, 'I need a drink. Come on!'

She grabbed my hand and led me off down the street.

I glanced back and had my final look at Ray's Video Emporium.

38.

Lindsay flagged down a taxi and we rode back into town. I told her that I didn't have any money, either to contribute for the taxi or even buy a drink at the pub, but Lindsay waved my plea of poverty away.

We sat in relative silence in the back of the taxi, Lindsay only really speaking to the driver, giving him directions to The Blessington Carriage, or The Bless, as it was known to pretty much everyone in Derby.

The traffic was heavy as we approached the town centre and we sat for a good ten minutes queuing to join the ring road. Neither of us spoke and it felt like a long time before we were moving again. Lindsay told the driver which lane to join (I felt sure the guy already knew where he was going) and which turning to take. He took Chapel Street as instructed and came to an abrupt stop right outside The Bless. Lindsay paid the driver, who didn't bother to thank her (in fact, he hadn't said one word the entire journey), and we both jumped out: me getting out the driver's side. The taxi was off down the road before I even reached the pavement.

It was now full dark and had dropped bitterly cold. I could hear The Smiths' 'Hand in Glove' blasting out from the pub. We hurried inside.

39.

The Bless had been the first pub I'd ever entered with the express intent of drinking. That was when I was fifteen, and I remember being astonished when they'd served me without question. I'd been in pubs before that, of course, but with my parents, and those occasions had mainly consisted of being given a bottle of Panda pop and a bag of crisps and told to 'go off and play': code for 'leave us the fuck alone to drink in peace'. But that first time in The Bless had been a revelation. Perhaps we'd gotten served because we were with Mark, who was then sixteen, and had always looked far older than the rest of us anyway (he had a bit of bum fluff on his chin at the time as well), or maybe it was just the fact that The Bless was a haven for young kids and the owners didn't give a fuck. Who knows? We got served anyway, and continued to get served from then on in.

The barmaids weren't too much older than us, and pretty much all of them were fit. One or two of the girls worked at Mercury Sounds as well, and one even had a job working weekdays in Video Magic. I'd been in once or twice to try and chat her up, but I'd been so nervous that the girl now believed I actually had a stammer.

Monday nights were when we usually went in. It was always packed and the music was always pretty good and there were always loads of girls. Students mostly. At last orders there was usually a mass exodus to the Rock House across town, where headbanging was the order of business. I'd even pulled in there once or twice. Paul claimed he'd fingered a girl on the dance floor once, but none of us believed him.

'Hand in Glove' gave way to 'New Rose' by The Damned and Lindsay headed straight for the bar. It was pretty dead, but then it was only five o'clock on a Thursday afternoon, I suppose. Lindsay asked me what I wanted, and I said, 'You sure?' and she said, 'Yes, it's fine. I think we both deserve a drink after today.'

I said, 'Okay. A pint of lager then please.'

A girl in a tight Blondie t-shirt and beads in her hair served Lindsay. Mark had tried to chat this particular barmaid up once and had received a drink in the face for his troubles. The girl glanced at me as she poured our drinks (Lindsay also had a pint) and I felt sure she remembered me from that night, but she didn't say anything.

Once we had our drinks, we went and sat at a table in the corner. The lights were low and Public Image Ltd's 'This Is Not a Love Song' blasted out. Lindsay looked at me, held up her pint and necked half of it in one gulp. I did the same, but didn't quite manage to down as much as her. She wiped her mouth. 'Fucking hell! I needed that.'

We sat in silence for a long while. I guess we both felt a little dazed. I listened to John Lydon and tried to make sense of the day's misadventures, but couldn't. I had trouble forming a coherent narrative; events just seemed jumbled up. Lindsay downed her pint and said, 'Want another?' gesturing to my half full glass.

'No, I'm okay, Linz.'

'You're having another,' she told me, and strode back to the bar. The same girl served her.

Public Image gave way to Killing Joke's 'The Wait' and Lindsay returned with two pints and a bag of dry roasted peanuts. She tore the bag down the middle and put them on the table so we could share. I took a handful.

'I can't believe those two fucking morons,' she said. I knew this was coming. 'I mean... what were they thinking?'

I had no answer.

'Mark always has to get involved,' she continued. 'He can't help himself. In the space of twenty-four hours he's got in two fights, once to stick up for you and then...today... for that twat mate of yours... gets his soddin' nose broken and then gets fuckin' arrested! You couldn't make it up.'

I had no idea what to say. She looked really pissed. I finished my first pint and immediately started on the second. I was beginning to regret coming to the pub with her.

'What is it with you lot?' she asked. 'All you seem to be interested in is all these stupid fuckin' films. Even Mark's addled over them. I mean, I like a good film, but you lot are obsessed. What is it?'

I wanted to tell her the truth. I wanted to tell her that horror films gave me a rush; that they fuelled me, inspired me to want to get out of this town and make something of myself. I wanted to tell her that I found a strange comfort in the mall in *Dawn of the Dead*, or in the sweltering dirt of *The Texas Chain Saw Massacre*, or in the suburban nightmare of *Halloween* – that they were landscapes in which I wanted to live (at least, in my imagination). I wanted to tell her that they guided me, made me understand I didn't have to fall in with any narrow-minded preconception of what I should be doing with my life; that there were men and women out there working on the fringes, creating macabre masterpieces that only a small number of people in the world understood, or even cared about (or so it seemed); that they had entrenched in me the idea to make independent films of my own, just like Sam Raimi and Rob Tapert and Bruce Campbell.

I wanted to tell her that they made me feel alive.

But I didn't.

Instead, I said, 'I dunno.'

40.

Four pints in and I was starting to feel pissed. I hadn't really eaten anything all day and Lindsay was knocking 'em back like tomorrow was an abstract concept, forcing me to keep up with her. Also, she was sitting close to me, talking into my ear. I was incredibly aware of every part of her body touching mine: her leg, her hip, her arm, and, when she touched my forearm to get my attention, her fingers. When she went to get a fifth pint (the one I knew would tip me over the edge), I had to adjust myself.

The Jam's 'In the City' was playing when she returned. She placed the glasses before us amongst our growing empties, and sat right up next to me. I glanced at her dark eyeliner and black lipstick and badly wanted to snog her. I got the distinct impression that she knew this. She leaned forward, rummaging about in her bag on the floor and her shirt rode up her back so I could see skin. Her arse looked fantastic in tight black jeans. I adjusted myself again.

She leaned back, a pack of cigarettes in one hand. She lit up and took a long drag. The smoke caught the low lighting and our corner of the pub suddenly looked decidedly *noir*-ish. She said, 'I remember when I was working at Mercury Sounds and you came in with Mark that day. You know, I thought you were both pretty fit.'

I think she clocked the total shock in my eyes, and she laughed and said, 'Oh, I shouldn't tell you that. You'll probably blab on me to Mark, won't ya?'

'No,' I blurted out.

She took another drag, then said, 'Funny how things turn out, isn't it?'

'Yeah,' I agreed, not entirely sure what she was referring to.

'I must have looked at bit of a state back then,' she said, 'I was full-on in my Siouxsie Sioux phase and doing a pretty poor job of it.'

'I thought you looked amazing,' I said. I could hardly believe this conversation was happening. I began to feel nervous.

'Really?' she said. 'Thanks, Scott. A girl needs to hear that sometimes.'

I took a long drink, downing almost half the pint, and wondered where the hell this was going. She turned to me. 'And what about now?'

'Now?'

'How do I look now?'

Total panic. I had no idea what to say.

I let the silence drag out a bit too long and she looked a little hurt. 'You don't have to say if you don't want.'

'No,' I said. 'It's not that. It's just… Mark's in the nick and we're here getting pissed and talking about…'

'Yeah, you're right. It's wrong.'

'Yeah. But.' I looked at her. 'I think you're well fit, Lindsay. You know that I do.'

She smiled. 'I liked that time at the Blue Note.'

'I thought we agreed we wouldn't bring that up ever again.'

I needed to get out of there before I did something really stupid.

41.

The Blue Note was probably Derby's biggest nightclub. Not in size, but in stature. Monday nights were for the Rock House, but Thursdays through to Saturdays, they were for the Blue Note. On Thursdays they had live bands on; I'd seen Thomson Twins, UB40 and Soft Cell there; not really my thing, but it was always a banging place, whatever night you went in (I felt a girl up in a dark corner during the Thomson Twins' set).

Even though the club itself was above some shops down Sadler Gate, there was something subterranean about it. Perhaps it felt that way because you had to enter it via a long, narrow passageway – I'd spent many a night queuing up down there to get in – and then once you were in, it was so dimly lit and cavernous you felt you *were* underground, even though you weren't. The dance floor was up a flight of stairs and, beyond that, another set of stairs led up to a long bar – always packed. There were no windows in the place. There was a back room that had a jukebox where you could choose your own stuff: no Maiden though. Plus, and much like The Bless, it was always full of students. The girls were incredible.

It'd been back in June when I'd got off with Lindsay. All four of us had been out since the beginning of the night. We'd had a few in Seymour's, then, as per, spent the rest of the night in The Bless. We were celebrating our forthcoming eviction from school. Well, Paul and I were anyway: Mark and Linz had already been left a year. We all got smashed pretty quickly. I know that Paul pushed a guy over by the pool tables in the backroom of The Bless and all his mates piled in on Paul and, of course, Mark stepped in and they were all chucked out by the bouncers. Lindsay was so pissed off she wouldn't go after them and I was too sozzled to think properly, so we stayed to play pool and drink some more, and before I knew it we were walking down Sadler Gate to the Blue Note, hand in hand.

We stood at the bar talking for ages; the music loud, the place rammed. Lindsay told me about her domineering parents and how they didn't get on and I was knocking back cans of Red Stripe, one after the other. She told me that when she was fourteen she had the sudden realisation that her parents weren't these great intellectuals and didn't, in fact, know everything, as they'd led her to believe; that they were just as fallible and as clueless as everyone else; that they were just winging it. In fact, she realised, their world-view was at best limited, and they were deeply ignorant about a great many things. I totally understood. She told me it had been a startling, and incredibly liberating, revelation. After that, any fear or power they may have had over her was gone. Obliterated. They became something different in her eyes. Their overbearing and demanding ways became something of a joke to her, and, she told me, she knew at fourteen that she wanted get out as soon as and experience as much as she possibly could. She said, 'I want to fill up on life' and I wanted to kiss her there and then.

Joy Division's 'New Dawn Fades' came on and she grabbed my hand and led me through a wall of bodies to the dance floor. She pressed herself against me and the feel of her and the yearning pull of Ian Curtis' voice made me close my eyes and I was completely in the moment. I don't think I'll ever forget it. Before the song was over, we were kissing.

42.

We agreed never to speak about what happened; a pact we made three days later when I went round to the Batcave. Mark had been in the shower and Lindsay and I had spoken in hushed voices in the kitchen. It had just been a kiss, but that had been enough to make me feel wretched (although not wretched enough to stop me from thinking about Lindsay pretty much constantly). After we left the Blue Note that night there had been a moment when I thought I might end up at the Batcave – the night certainly felt as if it was heading that way. But once we got outside, the night air must have sharpened our senses and the full weight of our illicit snog began to settle heavily in our stomachs and we parted ways in separate taxis.

Since our agreement, Lindsay and I had never once brought it up. Sure there had been glances pass between us, the odd time when our hands may have lingered upon one another for slightly longer than a polite greeting between friends should constitute, but, other than the seemingly endless fantasies and scenarios I played out in my head about us, we'd been as good as gold. That all changed that dark afternoon in The Bless. Lindsay really seemed up for it and that scared me. It scared me because I knew I had about as much willpower as an alcoholic in a distillery.

I wanted her.

Bad.

43.

I was plotting ways in which to leave when, quite suddenly, it began to chuck it down. Rain hammered against the pub's windows so loud it more or less drowned out Ian Dury and the Blockheads. Lindsay peered round the net curtain and pressed her nose against the glass. 'Bloody hell,' she said, 'it's tipping it down.' She sat back down. 'Might as well get another round in then.'

I was well pissed and horny as fuck; if she plied me with any more drink, I just knew I would make a move. Panicking, I said, 'Linz, I think we should get a taxi over to the police station. They might need us.'

She looked at me. 'Fuck 'em. Mark's made his bed time and time again. And that bellend mate of yours just cannot fuckin' help himself. They need to deal with it themselves.'

'Paul's alright,' I muttered.

'He's a fuckin' imbecile, Scott – an immature little boy.'

As much as I had a tendency to agree with her, at least some of the time, I felt I had to defend Paul. 'He's alright when you get him on his own.'

'Sure he is,' she said.

'He is. It's just when we're all out he tries to give it the big 'un.'

'It's all pretence with him, Scott. All an act. He's nowhere near as big and clever as he thinks he is.'

I sighed. 'Maybe so, but they're still our friends and we should be there for them.'

'Mark may well be my... boyfriend, but there's no love lost between me and Paul. I told Mark last night at the hospital that if he got himself into any more shit, then that would be it for us. And what does he do, not fuckin' twelve hours later...'

'But you saw what happened...' I said. 'I think it's sound that Mark always steps in to help us. He's just loyal. We're mates.'

'Yes, but he's the one that always comes off the worse for it.'

I couldn't argue with that and fell silent. Mark did seem

to have astonishingly bad luck. I finished my pint and the rain sounded like it had abated a little. Thin Lizzy's 'Jailbreak' came on.

If our impromptu drinking session had indeed been leading anywhere, I had destroyed it the moment I attempted to defend Paul. In fact, mentioning the lads at all appeared to harden Lindsay, and the flickering promise of getting off with her again now seemed well and truly gone. She looked angry, and sat there stewing, nursing the dregs of her lager. Just a few minutes before I had wanted to get the hell out of there before anything happened, yet now I knew anything happening was out the window I felt completely dejected, and somewhat confused. I longed for that electric charge between us; that pull of each other. It had gone in an instant and I suddenly found myself pissed off at Paul. We sat in silence for a long time.

Finally, Lindsay finished her drink and said, 'Let's go to the cop shop then.'

As soon as she said it I knew I didn't want to go.

44.

It was still pissing it down as we left the pub. Lindsay put her hood up and nuzzled her chin deep into her coat. My jacket didn't possess a hood, or a zip that worked all the way to the top, so I got drenched in seconds.

Wet jeans clinging to my legs and hair matted to my skull, we hurried in silence down Chapel Street, across the road, past The Dial – another bar we frequented from time to time – and headed into town.

A street full of cars sat idling, all trying to get out of the city, their headlights smeared in the rain. We passed Seymour's and then the Derby Library and Lindsay shouted over the noise of the traffic and the rain, 'There's a taxi rank outside Slick Chick' – a pub I'd never been in – and she ducked down a side street and I had to run to keep up with her.

I thought about the factory job at Chelful and how my dad would be at home waiting for me to tell him how making my application had gone. I thought about Jim at the Job Centre threatening to cut off my dole. I thought about Ray's Video Emporium being pretty much over. I thought about *The Evil Dead* slipping through our fingers. I thought about Paul and Mark being arrested.

I thought about how Lindsay felt against me that night in the Blue Note.

We turned another corner, and I saw, beneath the smudge of lights from a fish and chip shop, huddled in the doorway, each munching chips from a cone, Peroxide Lee and Fatty Teardrop. They saw me straight away.

45.

Could this day get any fucking better?

46.

Lee, a mouthful of chips: 'There's that piss-flap from last night.'

Teardrop, to me: 'Alright, cunt juice?'

Lindsay, to me: 'Do you know these people, Scott?'

Me: 'Err.'

Lee: 'This your girlfriend, Scott?'

Me: 'No.'

Lee: 'No, didn't think so. There's no way a wank stain like you could pull a split arse that tight.'

Lindsay, to Lee: 'You fuckin' what? A split arse?'

Lee: 'Yeah.'

Lindsay: 'Come here 'un say that.'

Me: 'Lindsay, don't.'

Lee: 'Gobby bitch, ain't ya.'

Lindsay: 'Who are these pricks, Scott?'

Me: 'From last night.'

That was it. More hell broke loose.

47.

I watched in amazement as Lindsay strode over to the two bellends and socked Peroxide Lee straight in the chops. I think more than anything surprise got the better of him and he stumbled back, his chips scattering to the rain. Even Fatty took a step away from her.

Lee put his hand to his mouth and pulled it away, finding blood on his fingers.

'You fuckin' dirty twat,' he said, astonished by the turn of events.

Lindsay said nothing. She pulled her hood down and turned and walked back to me, the rain pelting her face.

'Come on,' she said.

'Oi! Come here. I'll fuckin' do ya.'

Neither of us looked back.

We turned the corner and that was when we heard them running after us.

48.

'Leg it!' Lindsay shouted, and I did. I was out into the road – an oncoming car blaring its horn – and across the street, my heart booming, before I chanced a glance behind. Lee was hard on my tail, Teardrop a little way behind him. Of Lindsay there was no sign.

That was when I really started to panic.

I took the hill up Green Lane, up past the old Hippodrome and the Metro Cinema. I'd seen Russ Meyer's *Faster Pussycat, Kill! Kill!* and Ken Russell's *The Devils* there over the summer (took a girl to *The Devils*, never saw her again).

I got a stitch and was breathing through my arse. I looked back and saw that Peroxide had lost some ground, but was still coming, his teeth bloody, his face like a metal bolt. Teardrop, however, was totally out of the picture. No sign of him.

I took a left and raced past the Rock House – I could make out the thud and roar of 'Run to the Hills' and if I hadn't been breathing so hard I would've laughed.

The universe has a strange sense of humour sometimes.

When I got down to Confetti's nightclub, I looked back, but couldn't see Peroxide Lee. I slowed a little, relief already rising, then he appeared from behind an old Bedford van parked up across the street, coming straight for me.

'You're fuckin' dead!'

I belted down Gower Street, past Sloanes, a pub in a converted church, and back down Green Lane. Full circle.

I made for the abandoned shopping precinct, hoping to lose my pursuer within its dark network of decay. From the street, I took a stairwell which zigzagged down into a concrete underpass and out into the precinct's midway. Black and silent shop fronts, carcasses all, stood apocalyptic in the driving rain. I heard Lee coming down behind me, his footfalls echoing about the precinct. I looked back. Figures were huddled around the underpass, eyes looking from me to the stairwell and the advancing peroxide prick.

I made for the shop to my left. Its door was hanging off and I slipped right on in, blackness swallowing me up.

The place looked to have been a butchers and it was seriously rank. I had to stop myself from gagging. There were the remains of a counter and beyond it hooks still hung from the ceiling. It made my skin crawl. I thought of *The Texas Chain Saw Massacre*.

Peroxide Lee was in the precinct. I ducked down and tried desperately to steady my breathing. It was ragged and heavy. The stitch in my side was killing me.

With one eye, I peered out through the corner of the shop's window. Much of the glass was boarded up, and the parts that weren't were sprayed in graffiti, so, as I'd also obscured most of my face behind its paint-peeled frame, I felt as concealed as could be.

Lee was out on the midway, turning about wildly. The rain came down in great droves, making a hell of a racket as it hit that forgotten place.

'Come out!' he shouted, as if that would convince me.

I watched him, crouched, my knees aching, wondering how the fuck I'd gone from being in The Bless flirting with Lindsay (or, more to the point, having Lindsay flirt with me), to being here, back in this stinking precinct for the second time in a day, shivering beneath a piss-storm sky, about to get battered by this cockend.

'Come on!'

He was going along the row of shops on the other side of the precinct, moving away from me, peering in any openings he could find. He seemed reluctant to actually enter any of the buildings though, and after inspecting three or four shop fronts, he walked back into the centre of the midway.

He looked down to the street at the other end of precinct. He hollered, 'Oi!' but it wasn't directed at me. I pressed my face against the glass and tried to see down to the street. I could just make out the lights of an Indian restaurant, but little else.

'Oi!' he yelled again. 'Drakie!'

I heard a voice shout back, 'Where'd he go?'

Fatty Teardrop came lumbering up the precinct. My stomach hit my anus.

'Fucker's hiding in here somewhere,' Peroxide said.

'You checked all the shops?'

'Have I fuck. Can't see nothing. Fucked if I'm going in

them. There's a load of bockers down them stairs back there as well. Who the fuck knows what's in the shops.'

'Well what we gonna do? It's pissing down.'

'I know, knob shack. He's gotta come out some time.' Lee turned and raised his voice. 'Haven't ya, Scott?'

I groaned.

I heard Drakie say, 'You believe his fuckin' girlfriend?'

'Wasn't his girlfriend. I reckon it was that other prick's from last night – the one I smashed in the face.' He spat. 'That's what my split lip's all about.'

'Ah, right,' said Drakie. 'That explains it then. She fuckin' kicked me as I ran past. Right in the bastard shin. Killed.'

'Yeah. She tried to push me over, but I dodged her, didn't I.' This was a statement, not a question. Cocky twat. I got the feeling that this was all for my ears. 'I should've gone back 'un sparked her out, but I wanted to get this streak of piss too much.'

I rested my forehead against the glass and screwed my eyes up. I wondered where Lindsay was now, if she was still out in the rain looking for me. I doubted it. Lee and Drakie began to walk back in my direction. I heard Drakie say, 'She was pretty tidy though, wa'n't she?'

Lee returned, 'I wouldn't kick it out of bed.'

I caught something to my left shift in the dark. I gasped and scrabbled across the floor away from the shape. Glass crunched under me. I felt my right hand slice open. Outside, I heard Drakie say, 'What was that?'

A figure rose up; a black mass cut against the dark of the shop. It rasped an awful 'Get out!' A voice guttural and made of hard years. The figure lunged for me and I reeled back and went crashing out the door and back into the precinct.

49.

The fatal mistake I made was losing my footing. I went straight over, scraping the backs of my hands and smacking my left knee on the concrete. The rain was relentless and so, in turn, were Lee and Drakie's boots.

I curled up into a tight ball and they kicked fuck out of me. One pointy boot struck me right on the coccyx and it fucking killed. Another, straight in the ear. One came down on my ankle and I screamed. It felt like an anvil dropping on me from a great height. My mind flashed on Wile E. Coyote, but other than that, I thought about nothing at all. There was nothing other than the pain.

I heard them laughing and jeering, and I think that was when I began to cry. Also, I began to plead with them to stop, but I can't be sure now if I actually managed to vocalise this or if it was just in my head. And as for how long this kicking went on for, I cannot say either. It seemed like an age, but in reality it was probably not very long at all.

With my eyes screwed tight, and my head tucked deep into my arms, I had little to no perception of the actual events. I do remember the sounds, however. The thudding and scraping of soles about the wet ground; the dull boom in my skull that came with each and every kick; the rain: its steady, rhythmic clatter, and my own lamentations, unrestrained and surprising to my own ears.

Then, from far off in the distance, I heard a voice shout, ''Ere! Give over!'

There was a scuffling of feet and the kicks came no more. I heard Lee say, 'Come on,' and they both fled, their boots thumping and splashing away down the precinct.

I remained curled in a ball. The rain fell on me and it felt good, although bitterly cold. I heard footfalls approaching, but I dared not move. I sobbed, and heard a loud ringing in my ears. My entire body throbbed; I felt huge, elephantine, as if I had become bulbous with inflamed limbs and grotesque deformities. I wondered if any bones were broken and how much blood was leaking from me. I wondered if I would be able to walk out of this grim precinct, or have to be carried out.

I wondered how the day could get any worse.

50.

I eased myself over and watched the rain come down from the black and starless sky above. I thought about the time when Mark and I went into Mercury Sounds and first saw Lindsay. She was circling the store, filing records, looking like Siouxsie Sioux in thick-black eyeliner, torn t-shirt and frilly black skirt, tights laddered to fuck, painted Doc Martens. We both noticed her right away.

That day I bought Pink Floyd's *Meddle* and Mark picked up Judas Priest's 'Breaking the Law' on 7". We chatted to Linz for quite a while. We both got on with her instantly. Her hair was longer then, and fell down into her face. I fancied her immediately. So did Mark. He told me as much when we were leaving the record store, and so, I kept my own feelings to myself.

We saw her a few nights later in the Rock House. Mark got off with her that night and I got so pissed I spewed up on the side of the dance floor and fell headfirst, sparked out, into my own puke. I was woken shortly after by a bouncer and kicked out: Paul, Mark, and even Lindsay, all laughing at me as I was led staggering from the club.

As I lay in that derelict place, watching the rain fall to earth, my body a network of hurt, I wondered if all this was not karma; penance for how I'd betrayed Mark, who was still oblivious. I felt utterly wretched.

Footfalls approached. I tensed up, yet still couldn't find the will (or the strength perhaps) to move. My view of the black night and its hard rain was broken by several faces that appeared around me, all peering down. Five men. Bockers all.

'Y'areet, lad?' one of them asked.

I looked at him. He was filthy, of course, but had a kind face, and, I was surprised to find, I recognised him immediately. He had been the tramp that Paul had shouted 'Bocker' at earlier in this very precinct. That felt like days ago.

'I think so,' I said.

'You got a right good drumming,' another said, one with a wiry beard.

The kindly looking tramp said, 'Can ya stand, lad?'

'I don't know,' I said, and tried to sit up, wincing at the pain in my stomach and at a real sharp pain in my lower back. These low men took me from under my arms and lifted me gently. I got to my feet and they let go and I stood looking at them. I felt a little dizzy, but otherwise seemed to be intact.

'Why were those lads raggin' on you,' asked the one with the beard.

I answered honestly. 'I don't really know.'

'We got some Special Brew under them there stairs, my lad,' said the kindly tramp.

'I'm good,' I said, but part of me was tempted to join them; I would've liked to have found out who these men were and how and why fortune had led them to living in an abandoned shopping precinct. But I didn't. Instead, I said, 'I've gotta go.'

The kindly one looked at me. He really didn't look like he belonged in so low a place. 'Well… you do what you gotta do, I suppose,' he said. 'Just you look after yoursen.'

'I will,' I said. 'And thanks.'

'No worries, youngun. Just stay out of trouble. You shouldn't be bleeding down here with the rest of us.'

I looked at him and saw that he was deadly serious. I shivered and got the hell out of there. Limping all the way.

51.

It stopped raining. The lights of shop fronts reflected in great puddles, insipid yellows and reds and glaring whites; car tyres knifed through the slick on the roads. People appeared from bus shelters and door fronts and buildings dripped and the night air smelt clean. The city shaking off the storm.

I wandered through the town, past the Eagle Centre, heading towards home. The thought of which filled me with dread. I hurt, but nowhere near as much as I imagined I would. My ankle killed, but the other aches and pains were tolerable. I figured that my body must be bruised in certain places as several areas were tender to the touch.

Piles of sodden leaves lined the pavements and home seemed such a long way to walk. My head felt foggy, and all I wanted to do was lie in a hot bath for hours. I knew there was no chance of me doing that, of course. The interrogation from my folks about how I'd got into such a state, and, of course, how my application to work at the toy factory went, would have to be negotiated before I could even think about heading to my room, or the bathroom for that matter.

My socks squelched in my trainers and I began to notice a pain in my right hand. I saw a long gash across the palm and I remembered cutting it trying to escape the bocker in the butchers. There were other scrapes and nicks on both my hands as well, and a nice purpling bruise on my left wrist. I hadn't even felt that one until I saw it. I prodded it gently and found it was incredibly tender.

Then I remembered something and drove my wounded hands into each of my front pockets. I found the piece of paper and pulled it free. It was soaking and I opened it up carefully. The ink had run and what I had written was almost illegible. I would have to try and rewrite it out as soon as I got home, before I forgot it; knowing full well that *as soon as I got home* just wasn't going to happen. I considered going to Paul's to do it and then remembered he'd been arrested, and even if he'd been let out by now, his parents would in no way appreciate my visit.

I wondered what time it was; I had no idea. I looked to

the sky, past the great trees that lined London Road. There was a dark slate of cloud, no gap to the universe beyond. I wondered if it might rain again. The Derby Royal Infirmary was lit up to my right and I thought of Mark and Lindsay in there until the early hours of this hellish day. Its Victorian structure looked ominous in the night.

I was dazed from the entire day. Little of it made much sense. I felt like crying again, but held my tears back.

I walked the long mile or so down London Road going over and over the events of the day. Analysing things I'd said and done, wishing I'd done and said things differently. The events which played so heavily on my mind were me and Lindsay in The Bless, the kicking I'd got in the precinct (no question), and what went down at the video shop. Each exciting instalment filled me with swarming anxiety.

By the time I got to Alvaston, my ankle felt inflamed and I could hardly put any weight on it. Still, I turned off London Road and cut down Rugby Street towards Wilmorton College. I just couldn't face home. Not yet.

52.

The dark and silent blocks of the college stood tall against the night. There was a light on in one of the stairwells which wound up and up several storeys. Other than this illumination, the place was in utter darkness. I hobbled along the cycle track and headed for Alvaston Park. I avoided the grass – a quagmire after the storm – and took the narrowed path around the green, taking me along the back of the college. The wind picked up, but the leaves hardly stirred, wet and clumped as they were. The trees spoke though, cackling away above me. I could hear the road from across the green and looked over to its flare; the white and red of car lights and the ugly yellow of street lamps, all colours bleeding and shifting. I needed to sit down.

I followed the path away from the college and past eerie tennis courts until I got to the children's playground in the centre of the park. I sat on one of the swings and contemplated my existence.

Surmising that it was shit.

53.

I must have sat there for a good half an hour or more. The rest eased my ankle and gave me time to process all that had happened, and it allowed me to mentally prepare myself for the onslaught from my parents, particularly my dad. It was just nice to be still for a while. Above the college, the clouds finally broke and revealed the October moon. It threw silver on the merry-go-round and monkey bars and for the first time in a long time I found myself at a strange sense of peace.

Did any of this even matter?

My life that is. All this worry and anxiety, and for what? I was nothing but molecules and atoms and stardust; a conscious grain of sand, blowing in the universe for a brief spark of time, with only a one way ticket to the dirt as an absolute. I found something strangely comforting in this melancholia; until that moment, I had never thought about my existence in such a way. I found it liberating. Something shifted in my perspective; my consciousness realigned. Why should I be so scared all the time? Why should I not fully embrace who I was and the things I wanted to do with my life? Surely the entire journey should be played my way. I was the one checking out at the end. I'd got to feel good about what I did.

I sat there for a long time.

Dark and slivery wisps of cloud crossed the face of the moon and after a while I decided to go home and tell my dad exactly what he could do with the job at the toy factory.

54.

It didn't go well.

55.

At all.

56.

They were watching the news when I got in. When she saw me, my mum leaped up from off the settee. 'Lord almighty, what have you been doing?'

I just shrugged.

Dad didn't even look round from his chair in front of the telly. 'What time do you call this?' he asked, eyes fixed on a piece about Ronald Reagan meeting Colonel Gaddafi, all smiles and extended handshakes.

'Dunno,' I muttered.

'Well, your mum made you dinner,' he said, still not turning round. 'You could have had the decency to call her and tell you wouldn't be back.'

'I didn't have any money for the phone box.'

'I wonder why that is,' he said.

Mum said, 'What have you been doing? You look like a drowned rat... and you're filthy...' She inspected my arms, pulling my sleeves up a little. 'And what are these? Have you been fighting?'

Dad turned round.

On the telly, the Reagan piece ended and it cut back to the studio and some newsreader started talking and I heard the words *Video Nasties*. Dad got up out of his chair and came over to inspect me. I had both of them looking me up and down, Mum pulling my sleeves up again to show Dad my bruises, then clocking the cuts on my hands, particularly the deep gash across my palm.

'What on earth have you been doing?' said Dad.

Some MP was being interviewed and I tried to listen. 'We are talking about scenes that are really horrific,' this guy was saying, 'and leave nothing to the imagination: mutilated bodies, cannibalism, gang rape... that is what a video nasty is.'

'Well?' pressed my dad. 'Someone duff you up?'

'No, Dad,' I said, tilting my head to see past him. Now there was a shot of two young boys on the TV shoving a copy of *Cannibal Holocaust* into a Betamax. The voiceover said, 'It doesn't seem believable, yet everyday this is what scores of

Britain's school-children are up to. They're tuning in in their thousands to the sickening violence of an endless stream of video nasties.'

'Well, you've clearly been doing something,' said Mum. 'Look at you!'

'Out with it, lad.'

I missed the next part of the news report because of Mum and Dad's relentless questions, but I did clock some old woman being interviewed. A caption came up that told this was Mary Whitehouse.

'Look at us when we're talking to you,' said Mum.

'How did you get those bruises, Scott?' said Dad. I could see he was quickly losing his patience.

'... public concern about the proliferation of these kinds of videos has been fuelled by a powerful press campaign.'

'Scott!' my dad snapped. 'Never mind the box! Start talking.'

'There's nothing to say,' I muttered.

'... they only relate to violence, and it's violence for violence's sake that the police are opposed to.'

'I think there's a lot to say, my lad,' said Dad. 'Now out with it!'

'... an extravaganza of gory violence, capable of depraving and corrupting those who watch it...'

'Scott, please talk to us,' said Mum.

I kept missing things people were saying on the news and I was getting more and more wound up. Again, Dad tried to get my attention. 'Scott!'

On the screen, the MP who'd been on before was talking again. I caught his name this time: Graham Bright, a Conservative backbencher. He said, 'I believe that research is taking place and it *will* show that these films not only affect young people, but, I believe, they affect dogs as well.'

That was when I snapped. 'What do you want me to say?'

They didn't answer. My aggression certainly surprised my mum. 'You want me to say that I got me head kicked in tonight... that I got ragged round Duckworth Square by a couple of inbreds. Is that what you want to hear?'

'Is that true, Scott?' asked Dad.

'No, I just made it up. I done these cuts and bruises to myself. But don't worry if I'm alright or anythin'...'

'Oh, Scott,' said Mum. She looked really upset, but I was too angry to care.

'Just lower your tone there, boy,' said Dad.

'Why? So I can listen to you go on and on about what a shit son I am? How the only thing you want for me is to work in some wank job and go nowhere? About how I'm a complete waste of space...'

'Scott.'

'No, Dad, you listen. I'm sick of being judged all the time. Do you really think that's gonna motivate me to do any-thing... anything at all? I'm my own person, with my own ideas, and I will live my life how I want to.'

'Scott, listen to yourself,' said Dad. 'You're being very childish.'

'Fuck you.'

That was the moment I knew I'd gone too far. They were both stunned. In fact, it was more than that. They both looked incredibly hurt, particularly Dad.

'Oh, fuck this,' I said, and stormed out of the room.

'Scott!' cried Dad.

I grabbed my sodden jacket from the banister and rushed to the front door. Mum and Dad spilled out into the hall. I opened the door.

'Scott, don't go,' said Mum. She was bawling now.

Dad looked at me as if I were a stranger to him.

I slammed the door behind me.

57.

I went and pulled wing mirrors this way and that and bent and snapped off car aerials. I kicked over bins and stamped on flowerbeds. The streets were pretty quiet and my path of destruction made a right clatter, but I didn't give a shit. I stormed about pretty aimlessly at first, taking dimly lit backstreets and the odd jitty. A few houses had carved pumpkins in their windows; crooked-toothed jacks flickering with candleflame, and they seemed to be laughing at me. I came across two or three pumpkins on front steps, or on garden walls. I kicked these into the road.

These little vandalic flourishes were done out of pretence more than anything. I could already feel my anger ebbing away. Guilt was replacing it: a strong, all-encompassing guilt that made me want to throw up. The last pumpkin I annihilated was simply to try and hold on to the anger. The anger felt good; it gave me a rush, and a purpose. But the guilt was flooding me.

I took Bolton Lane and headed up to my old school. My junior school to be exact. I passed the graveyard where we all used to hang out smoking and drinking back in secondary school and then cut down a side street. A dog was barking somewhere in the distance and the moon reappeared from behind shreds of metallic cloud.

I felt so low, and so lost.

58.

I scaled the iron railings and dropped down, as carefully as I could, into the old playground. It killed my ankle. I could make out crude hopscotch patterns chalked on the ground and I remembered playing British Bulldog in this playground and Steve Hasse elbowing me in the face and giving me a nosebleed. He got done for that.

The school looked far smaller than I remembered it. But then I was, of course, a little person when last in this place. The moon rode the billowing sky above the old classrooms and I limped across the playground. I recalled each and every room, particularly the one where Mrs Cope poked me repeatedly in the ribs with her pen for struggling to read out aloud from some book.

I peered into dark windows. Here was the hallway leading down the rows of classrooms. There were bookcases and coat pegs set at low levels and small plastic seats and I wondered if I was really the same person who once came to this school. It seemed so long ago, and yet, at the same time, it didn't. Each window I peered in felt familiar and sparked a new memory, unthought-of for years, perhaps since the actual event in question. I recalled faces and teachers and friends I once had. I recall the first girl I liked, Donna Scaffe, and us holding hands out on the playing field behind the school and both of us thinking it was really naughty. I recalled doing my cycling proficiency and falling off over and over again and the entire class pissing themselves laughing at me and us all getting into trouble. I recalled Mrs Wood teaching us about the Great Fire of London and learning who Adolf Hitler was and why we had Guy Fawkes' Night. I recalled hating Maths, but enjoying English, and writing my first (and only) poem one Halloween. It was about a plastic skeleton that hung at the back of our class. His name had been Herbert. I still remember it. It went:

> A skeleton is a bony thing,
>
> A skeleton is a thin thing,
>
> A skeleton has no brain,

He cannot think,
He cannot blink,
He has no eyes to see you with.
But Herbert here's a nice old chap,
Who hangs around all day... perhaps?

I recalled my teacher at the time, Mrs Pritchard, telling me the poem was really good and making me stand up in assembly to read it and me not being able to say skeleton properly – instead pronouncing it *skelington* – and muttering and shaking through the entire reading. They even brought old Herbert out to stand with me. The entire school clapped afterwards though and I buzzed off that.

I peered into that old assembly hall, which also doubled as the school gym, and I saw that the great song sheets still hung from the back walls. Boys and girls used to have to take it in turns to stand up in front of assembly and turn those great sheets of paper over onto the next song. They were really heavy. We'd sing three or four each morning, all stood in uniformed rows. *The ink is black, the page is white, together we learn to read and write... to read and write.* And, *Dance, dance, wherever you may be, for I am the Lord of the Dance, said He.* And, *Morning Has Broken* and *Jerusalem*, and other such classics.

I continued round to the back of the school.

The playing field was moon-washed and I sat on a wall and watched shadows shift in the breeze. I thought about telling my dad to fuck off and the look on his face before I slammed the front door. I put my head in my hands and wondered if I even knew who I was.

59.

Paul was smashing in Carl's beloved Mark II Escort.

After Bolton Juniors I drifted back into the night and almost instinctively headed for Paul's. Lost in my own thoughts, I didn't even realise that was where I was heading until I was pretty much there. I turned into his street and could hear the breaking of glass. Then I heard a dull thud. I walked up the road, hearing more and more clatterings and bangings, and about halfway up I caught sight of a figure moving around a car. I recognised the motor before I recognised Paul. The ill yellow of street lamps illuminated the puke green of Carl's Ford Escort in a ghastly way. Then I saw Paul. He was holding a cricket bat and muttering profanities. How no one had heard this racket was beyond me, but then I guess it was getting pretty late (I had no idea of the actual time) and most houses were dark and still, save for the odd flickering of a television set and a few bedroom curtains lit up bright. I saw Paul hold the bat high above his head, readying to smash in the windscreen. He fixed himself in that position for a moment – I guess willing himself to do the deed – and framed in that street yellow of night he'd looked almost cinematic; a cut-black figure dealing out terrible vengeance. I thought it would make a great shot in a movie.

Before that cricket bat connected with the windscreen, and put Paul way, way beyond the point of no return, I called his name. He looked round, startled, and dropped the bat. It hit the road and the hollow knock echoed about the houses. A curtain twitched to my left. I thought Paul was going to run for it, but then he saw it was me.

'Bradley?'

'Yeah.'

'Fuck you doin' here?'

I didn't answer. I made my way over and inspected the damage to his brother's car. Both headlamps were smashed in and there was a dint in the bonnet, but other than that, it looked okay, at least by the street light. I glanced at Paul's house. It was all dark.

'No one's in,' he said.

'Where's Carl?'

'Still at work.'

'Your Mum and Dad?'

'Fucked off to the pub. Said they've washed their hands of me.'

I turned to Paul. His eyes were all bloodshot and his hands were trembling.

'You okay?' I asked.

'Do I fuckin' look okay?'

'No.'

'Well then.'

'What happened?'

Paul just shook his head. Tears welled in his eyes. He leaned against his brother's Escort and said, 'I wish there was a pause button, y'know...'

'What?' I said, the weight of his emotion taking me by surprise.

'On life. I wish there was a fuckin' pause button.' He started to cry. I had never seen him like this.

'A pause button?' I said.

'Yeah. It's just exhausting. Day after fuckin' day. No chance to catch up...' He looked right at me and said, 'I can hardly breathe.'

I avoided his eyes and looked at the bat in the road.

'Don't you feel it?' he said, his words heavy.

'What?'

'*What?* That fucking dread? It's relentless.'

'I don't know,' I said, although I did know.

He stared at me. 'I'm exhausted by life. Every day I have to get out of bed... and for what?' He let that hang and wiped his eyes. I heard an owl hoot somewhere in the night. Paul said, 'I don't know what I'm gonna do.'

We fell silent. A car went by on the main road at the bottom of the street. We both watched it pass.

'I went down to our old school,' I said.

'Noel Baker?'

'No. Bolton.'

'Ain't been down there in ages,' he said.

'Nor 'ave I. It's still the same. Only smaller.'

He gave a thin smile. I looked at him and said, 'I feel it too, mate. It's like I'm just existing... waiting for my life to start. Only… I don't know how it ever will. Everything feels like a dead end.'

Paul looked at me. I found it difficult to read him, but I think he found a truth in what I'd said, and in that, a comfort that someone else understood. At that moment I felt closer to him than I ever had.

He said, 'We need to get outta here and find Mark.'

'Why?' I said.

He smiled. 'Because I think there's a way we can get our copy of *The Evil Dead* back.'

60.

We started walking and that was when the police car turned into the street. Paul grabbed my arm. 'Fuck! A Panda!' he said, and legged it down the side of someone's house. He was over their side gate like lightning. I ducked down behind a parked car and wondered what the hell to do. The police car slowly slid up the street, its headlights arcing across the houses. I looked to the gate Paul had scrambled over and saw him peering back at me. 'Come on!' he whispered as loud as he dared.

The police were getting close. Still bent down low, I hurried down the side of the house making for the gate. Paul's face was no longer peering over and all of a sudden I felt completely alone and utterly exposed.

I scrambled up onto the gate, my feet scraping down the front trying desperately to find some purchase, straining to pull myself up by my arms. I heard the car stop behind me and that was when I got really scared.

Before the shouting started, I saw (and *felt*) great waves of blue light probe me. A voice shouted, 'You! Stop!' and I felt like I was in a film. I heard Paul call out a desperate, 'Come on!' and I heard hard boots running up behind me.

My foot found the latch and I flung myself up and over the gate. I leapt down into the garden and yelped at the pain in my ankle and I saw Paul stood looking frantic on the edge of a large moonlit lawn. A police officer hit the gate behind me and I looked up and saw fingers spidering along the top searching for a grip. I looked back at Paul and he shouted, 'RUN!' and we did. We were across that lawn and over a fence and into the next door's garden in no time at all. These gardens were our domain.

Back in the day, Paul and I used to go cat creeping. At least, that's what we called it. When I used to crash over, which was often, we'd wait until his parents had gone to bed and then sneak out into the night, usually armed with a 10p mix and a fag – stolen from his mum's handbag – and 'creep' through the gardens. We'd keep to the edge of properties, and as the gardens on Paul's street were fairly long, we'd be, for the most, well hidden from view from the backs of people's houses. The thrill of getting caught was always exhilarating and we'd often get a fit of the giggles from the sheer gall of our daring. We'd find a nice shed roof or something and look at the night sky and share the cigarette and eat all the sweets. For 10p you could get twenty half-penny chews. We never once got caught.

We'd not been cat creeping since we were about thirteen, but those gardens all felt familiar still and we pretty much knew every gap and cushy route and we lost the titheads fast. The adrenaline numbed the pain in my ankle. We slipped down a jitty and out onto the main road, ran across that, and slipped behind the social club and caught our breaths.

We looked at each other and laughed. Paul said, 'Man… what a fuckin' day.'

'You're not wrong there, mate. That was close.'

'Fuckin' was. Lindsay told us you got chased earlier by them two cockends from last night.'

I looked at him. 'You saw Lindsay?'

'Yeah. She came to the station just as we were being let out.'

'Really?'

'Yeah. And Mark's not happy with you.'

My stomach knotted. 'Why?'

'Cause Linz told us you two went straight down The Bless after we were arrested.'

'Oh.'

'Mark and Linz had a right barney. Me mum and dad were there and it was well embarrassing. Lindsay pretty much dumped him on the steps right outside the police station. And it was fuckin' raining. It was right miserable.'

'They split up?'

'Think so. Mum and Dad dragged me back here and left 'em to it, but it certainly looked that way when I was leaving.'

'Jesus.'

'That's not the half of it, Scott. Come on, let's get movin' and I'll fill ya in.'

61.

So Paul gave me the low-down on his time spent at the pleasure of the Derbyshire Constabulary and I was amazed, and relieved, to find that he and Mark had been let off with a caution. 'Not before a right round of fucks from that prick Moir though,' explained Paul. 'And my twat of a brother. He fuckin' loved it. The cunt.'

Ray Ellis hadn't fared so well. Paul reckoned he had been well and truly booked and had even been given a court date for sometime in November. 'He might go down,' said Paul, and I believed him.

We walked through the night. It was late and it was quiet. There were only a few cars on the road and hardly anyone about. I wondered if my parents had gone to bed or if they were waiting up for me. I knew I wouldn't be going home tonight.

I told Paul about my kicking at the shopping precinct and Paul said we would have to get them back. He looked really pissed off and it made me feel good that he cared.

We headed into Allenton and crossed the spider bridge – so-called because it arched arachnid-like above the roundabout below – and we took one of several walkways down into the shops. We saw a chippy open and Paul ducked in and bought us both a bag of chips. He had a pea mix, actually, and I had a chip cob. Until I began eating I hadn't realised how hungry I was. I started to wolf it down, and holding the bag warmed my hands up.

While we walked and ate, Paul said, 'You know what?'

'What?' I mumbled, my mouth full.

'In a hundred years, no one will give a shit 'bout any of this.'

'What ya mean?'

'All this shit that's going on, man – no one will care.'

'Suppose.'

'Think about it. We'll be long gone. Worm food.'

'Cheery.'

'What I mean is… should we really be worrying about any of this? Does any of it even matter?'

I didn't answer. I wasn't sure I had an answer.

Paul continued. 'I mean… I don't know what the fuck I'm doing. Days just drift into one another – nothing is clear anymore. But should I care? Maybe this is what life is – a series of random events interspersed with long stretches of shit.'

'Poetic.'

'You fuckin' know it.'

We walked on. Paul finished his pea mix and threw the paper to the ground. It blew about in the breeze. I finished my chips and did the same. Mine didn't blow about because I threw mine into the shop doorway of a Birds Bakery.

'You wanna hear my film idea?' I said.

'Your what?'

'I had an idea for a film.'

'Like a film film?'

'Yeah.'

'When?'

'Today. When we were all walking to Ray's and Lindsay was talking about the Black Death.'

'Wicked. Is it a horror?'

'Course.'

'Cool. What is it?'

'Well… it's about this deadly game of hide and seek.'

'Hide and seek?' He didn't sound impressed.

'Yeah,' I said, my confidence immediately wavering. 'There's this guy, or these bunch of guys, all dressed like them plague doctors Linz was on about and they go around kidnapping people and take them to this old, abandoned factory and then they make them play this deadly game of hide and seek.'

Paul was frowning. I went on. 'One of the plague doctors tells them the rules – they have five minutes or whatever to run and hide in the old factory and then the doctors come and search for them. If they make it through the night without being found, then they're free to go, but if they get caught…'

Paul's eyes lit up. 'Then it's slice and dice time?'

'Exactly. And all these doctors have loads of different weapons… knives and axes and stuff… to kill 'em with.'

'Why are they all dressed as plague doctors?' he asked, and for a moment I was stumped. All I could think of was because I thought they looked cool, but then I said, 'For disguise, and also because they're fuckin' frightening costumes. Plus, these guys see themselves as kind of righteous in what they're doing – like they're eradicating the world of a plague of scum. They see all the people they kidnap for the game as dirty, fucked-up people, and this is how they get rid of them.'

Paul actually seemed impressed and said, quite simply, 'Cool'. It was all I needed.

'What you thinking of calling it?'

'I don't know... "Hide and Seek" maybe?'

'What about "Run and Hide"?' offered Paul.

'Yeah, that's pretty cool.'

'You remember Black Death Beth in school?'

I laughed. 'Yeah.'

'You could have a character like her in it – a right bitch. She could be one of the ones they kidnap and she meets a right nasty end.'

'What made you think of her?'

'Just the name.'

'Oh, right. Not 'cause she blew you out that time then?'

'No. Fuck off.'

We walked on and Paul said, 'You could have loads of wicked death scenes.'

'Yeah.'

'It's like the perfect set up. Could be ace, Scott.'

'Cheers.' It felt really good to hear this. I said, 'Got an idea for the end as well.'

'What is it?'

'Well like... the main character actually survives the night and in the morning they let her go, but just as she's leaving another bunch of kidnap victims arrive ready for the next game and in among them is her parents.'

Paul thought about this, then said, 'Nah, not her parents. Be better if it was her boyfriend or something.'

'Yeah. Okay.'

'Whoa... Just thought of a well wicked title for it,' said Paul.

'What?'

'What about...' he paused for dramatic effect. 'Death Game?'

'Isn't that too much like *Game of Death*?'

'Alright then… what about, Factory of Death?'

'Yeah, that's pretty cool.'

'I know. You gotta have death in there, mate. Like *Faces of Death*.'

'Yeah, suppose. You like it then?'

'Yeah, man. I'd watch it. You gonna write it?'

'I think so.'

'Cool. Do it. Get outta this shit hole.'

'Yeah.'

We fell silent. I was buzzing off Paul's reaction to the idea and couldn't stop thinking about it.

When we turned down Mark's street, I said, 'You sure he's not gonna be at Lindsay's?'

'Not after the fight I saw,' said Paul. 'I doubt she'll let him round ever again.'

'Oh, right.'

I felt nervous about seeing Mark and hung back a little as Paul went through the front gate and made his way round the back of the house.

'Be quiet,' said Paul, even though I wasn't making any noise. 'His folks 'un little brother are probably in bed.'

'What time is it?' I asked, but Paul ignored me.

Round the back of the house we found curtains drawn, but lights on.

'Bet he's up watching telly,' said Paul.

'Could be his parents?'

'Nah, they go to bed at like half eight, don't they?' This was indeed true.

Paul gently tapped on the window. Nothing. He tapped again and suddenly the curtains twitched and out peered Mark. His face looked even worse than before. He had to squint to see out of his black eyes, then drew the curtains back and pointed to the back door. I could see he had the telly on.

Paul and I walked over to the back door and Mark let us in. It was warm inside. We grunted a few half-arsed greetings, then Mark said, 'I'll put the kettle on,' and busied himself doing just that.

'How's your nose?' I asked.

'Killing.'

'You got any tinnies?' Paul asked.

'No. Drank 'em all tonight.'

'Aren't you on pain killers?' I asked.

'Fuck them,' said Mark. 'I needed a drink.'

'Understandable,' said Paul. 'She dump you then?'

'Paul!' I said.

'What?' he said.

'Yeah she did,' said Mark, and I hated myself for feeling good about it.

'Well, you're better off, mate,' said Paul.

'Why am I?' said Mark.

Paul had no answer.

I cut in, 'Least you got let off at the cop shop.'

'Yeah,' he said. 'Just a caution. Fuckin' lucky. I thought we were screwed.'

The kettle boiled and Mark poured out three mugs.

'What you watching?' asked Paul, craning his head to see into the living room.

'Oh, I just threw *The Fog* on.'

'John Carpenter?'

'Yeah.'

I said, 'Adrienne Barbeau's well fit in that.'

'She's well old,' said Paul.

'She's fit though. You see her tits in *Escape from New York*?'

Paul pondered this, then said, 'True. They were quite spectacular.'

Mark handed us both a tea and we headed into the living room. The video was on pause. I knew the scene. It was the first big kill on the fishing trawler near the start of the film.

Paul said, 'This film is nowhere near as good as *Halloween*.'

'Suppose,' said Mark. 'It has its moments though.'

'*The Thing* is my favourite Carpenter,' I said, and Paul and Mark both agreed.

'He's got *Christine* coming out soon,' said Paul.

The conversation stalled and there was this weird moment where we just sat around and looked at one another. Then we laughed.

'What a fuckin' day,' said Mark.

'What a fuckin' day,' I agreed.

'One for the books,' said Paul.

We drank our tea and watched *The Fog*. After a few scenes, Paul admitted that Adrienne Barbeau was indeed well fit.

62.

We didn't watch the whole film. We sat in a kind of wounded silence for a little while; all of us running the day through our minds, trying to make some sense out of it. Then, after a somewhat animated debate – mainly on Paul's part – on who had the better tits: Jamie Lee Curtis or Adrienne Barbeau, I asked Mark what time it was. He went over to the gas fire and moved a few birthday cards – his little brother's – off the mantelpiece and revealed the clock. It was twenty to midnight.

I said, 'Man, today has seemed like forever.'

They both muttered in agreement. On the screen, Tom Atkins and Jamie Lee were heading out to sea to find the missing trawler.

Paul said, 'We gotta go soon.'

'Oh yeah,' I said. 'What's this plan? Where we goin'?'

'What plan?' asked Mark.

'Paul reckons he can get *The Evil Dead* back.'

Mark looked at Paul. 'Really?'

'Well, it's not for defo…'

'That prick Moir has probably had it destroyed by now,' said Mark.

'That's not what I heard,' said Paul.

'What you mean?'

'You know that lanky twat from today…'

'P.C. Spong?' said Mark.

'Yeah.'

'Yeah?'

'Well he told me something very interesting.'

'What?'

'He told me that all these videos go to some lock-up round Chester Green way and they have to watch them all… to establish whether or not they're fit for the general public. Can you fuckin' believe that?'

'No way?'

'Way.'

'When did he tell you this?' asked Mark.

'When you were in with Moir and I was out in the hallway. Spong came by and I started asking him what they did with all the films and he told me loads. He's alright, y'know.'

'What... when he's not grappling me to the floor and arresting us you mean?'

'Yeah.'

I cut in. 'So... all Ray's videos are in this lock-up in Chester Green?'

'Yeah. And loads more besides...'

'But if it's all locked up... how we gonna get in?'

'Spong told me that all the coppers fuckin' love it down there – they pull all-nighters and whack on all the films they've seized. Sounds fuckin' wicked, man.'

'Bollocks,' said Mark.

'Honest gods. That's what he told me.'

'He's gotta have been bullshittin' you.' I said.

'Why? What's so hard to believe?'

'Sound likes he was makin' it up,' said Mark.

Paul shook his head, exasperated. 'Well I'm gonna go down there to check it out. You can stay here if you want?'

'Why tonight?' said Mark.

'Cause Spong told me loads of 'em are going down there at midnight for a session. Said they get loads of tinnies in and 'ave a right laugh.'

'How are they getting away with that?' said Mark. 'What about Moir?'

'Spong reckoned that as long as all the paperwork is filled in... y'know, about each video... then they're pretty much left to just get on with it. And that's not all he told me either.'

'Go on then...'

'He said they make deals with "interested parties", as he put it, and they pirate copies for people.'

'Paul, mate, this has got to be a set up,' said Mark. 'We'll probably get down there and get arrested again.'

'Fuck sake, Jones. Stay here if you want, I don't give a shit, but I'm goin' down there. What you sayin', Bradley?'

They both looked at me. 'I want to believe it, Paul,' I said. 'I do. But... Mark's right, it does sound a little too good to be true.'

Paul sighed and put his head in his hands. On the screen, the fog was moving in from across the sea. Something occurred to me, and I said, 'Is Carl in on this?'

Paul grinned and said, 'No. They all fuckin' hate him. Think he's a right lick arse.'

We laughed. It broke the tension a little.

I said, 'What happened to him?'

'Dunno,' said Paul. 'He was always a bit of prick, but the police force has fuckin' changed him. Big time.'

'I'm sorry I doubted you, mate,' I said. 'He's a fuckin' giant prick now.'

'Yup.'

'He'll go spare when he sees his car.'

Mark said, 'His car?'

'Yeah,' I said. 'Found Paul earlier knocking fuck outta it.'

Mark laughed. 'His shit-green Escort?'

'Yeah.'

'Nice one.'

'Cheers,' said Paul. 'Look. Spong said they'd all be down there at twelve. I think we should at least check it out…'

I looked at Mark and Mark looked at me, then he rubbed his chin and said to Paul, 'Alright, fuck it. Let's go.'

63.

So we headed out into the witching hour. It was decided that Mark would front us for a taxi (we'd done enough walking for one day) and we marched off to the local taxi rank. None of us said much of anything. I think we were all pretty tired. My ankle had eased somewhat, but I could still feel it with each step and my sides and lower back were tender to the touch. I imagined that I was covered in bruises and the thought of wallowing in a long hot bath was still very much on my mind. Still, I'd decided to leave going home until the morning, once my dad had gone to work. I could handle Mum on her own, but not both of them together.

At the taxi rank we had to wait ten or so minutes for a cab to turn up. We stood beneath the neon glow of Western Cars in a huddle and tried to keep warm. I told Mark about my being done in by Peroxide Lee and his fat mate and Mark agreed with Paul that we would have to 'get them'. But for the most part, Mark was quiet and distracted. I guessed it was probably because of Lindsay and I wanted to say something to console my friend, but the entire situation just made my stomach knot up, so I didn't say anything.

The taxi pulled up and we all piled in. As we rode across Derby I thought about that night in the Blue Note and how Lindsay had felt against me and I wanted that again. Then I noticed Mark across from me, staring out of the window, and I felt really fucking low. Again, I wondered what kind of person I was and tried to think of something else entirely. My film idea, in point of fact.

Paul had come up with a pretty good title with "Factory of Death". But I wondered if that was the right way to go. I wanted a long title, something along the lines of *Last House on the Left* or *The Texas Chain Saw Massacre*, but the best I could come up with was "Come Play Games With Me", which was just awful, and sounded somewhat pederastic.

We pulled up on a dark, tree-lined street in Chester Green. Mark paid the driver and we all got out. The taxi reversed up, red brake lights spilling across the silent houses, and then rumbled off into the night.

With the vehicle gone, the quiet of the large expanse of Green fell in around us. Above the rustling trees, the moon rode the shreds and tatters of dark and silvery clouds, ever moving, ever changing.

Mark said, 'So where's this lock up then?'

And Paul said, 'Round the back of the old train buildings.'

So we cut across the Green and I wondered if I was living in a movie.

64.

The old British Rail buildings stood at the end of a torn up line; a towering hulk of a structure where, long ago, trains rolled in for maintenance and the tributaries of tracks led out into England. Now the tracks were all but gone, save for one broken line hidden beneath sprawling undergrowth, and the windows in the buildings were black holes and crumbling red brick was graffiti-scored. It was an ominous looking place. I thought it would make a good location for a horror film.

The three of us walked around the back and the moon was swallowed by black clouds and with the great structure blocking out the lights from the road beyond, the darkness was vast.

'There is fuck all out here,' said Mark. 'I can't see shit.'

'It's on the edge of the industrial estate,' said Paul, pointing into the dark. We couldn't see a thing, save for a few lights dotted out in the distance.

Mark tripped over something and nearly fell, but somehow managed to steady himself. 'This is fucking ridiculous,' he said. He had a point.

I was worried about going over on my ankle and made my way very carefully. I lagged behind and followed in their footsteps. Paul took the lead.

'Look!' Paul said, after a while. 'Check it out.'

Mark and I both looked. I made out lights spilling from a metal container unit on the edge of a lonely car park. Street lamps illuminated the road beyond. A few figures milled about.

'Told ya,' said Paul.

'You sure that's it?' I said.

'Yeah,' Paul answered. 'Must be.'

Mark said, 'Why di'n't we walk round on the road?'

'Cause it takes ages. You have to go right down to the bridge. Quicker this way.'

'You're a fucking mongol.'

We ascended a grass verge and stumbled out of the dark and onto the car park. The figures at the entrance of the container unit – more of a huge crate really, the kind used for international shipping – all turned and watched us approach.

I caught sight of the gangly shape of P.C. Spong and saw he was in plain clothes. Out of his uniform, he looked a lot younger. The figure next to him – a much larger and older man, still in police uniform – shouted across. 'Who's that?'

Paul spoke for us. 'We're looking for…err… P.C. Spong.'

I heard the large bloke chuckle.

'I'm here,' said Spong. 'That Mansell?'

'Yeah.'

We got closer and I could make out the inside of the unit. It was stacked with videos. I saw somebody moving about inside, then a face appeared at the doorway. It was P.C. Benton, who was also still in uniform. I suddenly felt very nervous.

The large bloke who had a cauliflower nose and bulbous eyes – he looked like a toad – said, 'Where did you lot come from?'

'From behind the old railway buildings,' said Paul.

'Fuck you come that way for?' You should've come round on the road.' He pointed to the street beyond.

'Dunno,' said Paul, shrugging. Mark gave him a right look.

Benton spoke up, 'What they doin' here?' I guess he was addressing Spong, but he stared at us. I looked at the ground.

'It's Mansell's brother,' said Spong, as if that answered everything.

'Know that.' Then to Paul he said, 'What's it like livin' with that prick?'

'Wank.'

'Can imagine.'

Suddenly, another face appeared from within the unit. I saw it was Colin, the Pirate Man. He saw me and said, 'Well, bloody hell. Like a bad penny you are. Your dad know you're out this late?'

'I don't know,' I said.

Colin had several tapes in his hands and Benton began looking at the labels. The toady looking bloke said, 'You know these kids, Col?'

The Pirate Man said, 'I know that one,' pointing to me. 'His dad's alright. He has tapes off me regular.'

Benton cut in. 'How many's that then... two, four... six...
that's a score, Col. Each.'

'Each! You're fuckin' joking aren't ya?'

'Price has gone up, Col. Risk goes up, price goes up.'

'He's right,' said Toady. 'I don't know how much longer
we'll be able to do this. Government's beginning to breathe
down our necks.'

'Why are all the tapes you seize stored here?' Mark asked.

'Because this has been a fuck up from day one,' Toady
said. 'We've been pretty much strong-armed into carrying out
raids. They've been happening all across the Midlands – all
across the country in point of fact – and we just haven't the
space at the station to store them all. We're inundated. So our
Serge had the bright idea of storing them all here. Even fitted
it out with a TV and video and told us to watch them all
and make detailed reports. Think the Serge thinks this entire
operation is bollocks... if you want my opinion.'

'You think he does, John?' said Spong.

'Well he doesn't seem overly concerned about this here
unit, does he? He just wants all the paperwork in so it looks
good for these government plebs.'

'What about Moir?' asked Mark.

'Moir was transferred down from Manchester. He pretty
much ransacked every video shop up there, so some bright
spark had the idea of bringing him down here. It's been a
friggin' nightmare ever since. Think our Serge would've let all
this bollocks go if it wasn't for him. Moir's well in with the
Festival of Light – those Whitehouse Bible bashers. Guy's a
clown.'

Behind this John fella, I heard Benton ask Colin if he was
having the tapes or not. The Pirate Man reluctantly handed
over the money and stepped from the unit.

To me, he said, 'Tell your dad I'll see him next month.'

'Yeah,' I muttered.

Then he said a 'See ya' to John – ignoring Spong – and
headed off into the night. John watched him go, then turned
back to us. 'Dan here said Moir brought you lot in yesterday.'

'Only me and Mark,' said Paul. 'Scott managed to evade
capture.' He nudged me.

Spong said to Mark, 'Sorry if we hurt your nose earlier.'

'You did, but...'

'Moir would make our lives hell if we're not seen to be upholding the law to the absolute utmost.'

'It's okay,' said Mark. 'It's done now.'

'Yeah,' said Benton. 'You two action heroes had to be put under control. What were you thinking?' There was good humour in his voice.

Both Paul and Mark shrugged.

Benton grinned. 'Right couple of Charlie Bronsons ain't ya,' then he added, 'Come on, let's give you the tour,' beckoning us inside.

65.

The unit was an Aladdin's Cave of VHS murder and mayhem. It seemed every conceivable horror title was either boxed, stacked or lined up on industrial shelving, often several times over. I clocked at least three or four copies of *The Last House on the Left* (I knew Paul would be clamouring for one of those), two copies of *Bloody Moon*, four or five *Don't Go in the Woods*, a *House By the Cemetery*, six *I Spit on Your Graves* and three *SS Experiment Love Camps*. And that was just in the one box closest to where I was standing. Written on the outside of said cardboard box, scrawled in black marker, was the word: *Seen*.

Paul and Mark stood either side of me. All our mouths were agog. Spong, Benton and John the Toad circled garden chairs positioned in the centre of the unit. A TV and video player had been put on a shelf by the back wall. Two standing lamps lit the scene. By the chairs, there were boxes of Skol lager and a six pack of Carling Black Label. And some Monster Munch.

'This is well wicked,' said Paul.

'You know it,' agreed Benton.

'Don't it get cold in here?' asked Mark.

'Nah,' said Benton. 'We've got a paraffin heater. Anyway, few lagers down ya neck 'un ya don't feel it.'

'Where you get the leckie?'

'We're hooked up. All mod cons.'

The three of us took to looking around, peering in boxes, and scanning the titles lined up on the shelves. John sat down in one of the garden chairs and cracked open a can of Skol.

Picking up a copy of *Zombie Flesh Eaters*, I said, 'What's gonna happen to all these videos?'

'Once we've written our reports,' said Spong, 'they'll most probably be destroyed. If they are deemed obscene that is.'

'Who decides that?'

Spong gave a shrug. 'We just fill in our reports,' he said. 'They're like questionnaires really. We tick boxes for the types of violence that feature in any given film. Sexual violence is

131

the kiss of death. A lot of these videos are already on the DPP list, so they'll be destroyed automatically anyway.'

'That's why we're making copies,' said John, swigging from his can.

'You're all crusaders,' said Paul. 'Fighting the system from within.'

John chuckled. 'If you like,' he said. 'Dan's the crusader. I'm just here to make a few bob on the side, I don't mind tellin' ya. Plus these films are a good crack.'

I ran my fingers along the spine of a line of videos. 'What's gonna happen to Ray Ellis?'

Spong glanced at Benton, then looked at me and said, 'I don't know. He might get off with a caution, but then…'

'He might get six months,' said Benton.

'Fella in Manchester got nine months,' John said.

We all fell silent for a moment, then Mark said, 'It's insane.'

'Nowt as queer as folk,' said John.

I peered into a box by my feet and there is was – the most ferociously original horror of the year, *The Evil Dead*.

I picked it up. The Holy Grail. The film that had become my obsession; the one that had led us on the merry dance of the last few days. I ran my finger across the cover, along the Palace Pictures logo and down the Candarian demon's face. Paul saw what I was holding and rushed over.

Spong noticed us and said, 'Yeah, that's one of the boxes from Ellis's.'

'This is mine,' said Paul.

''Fraid not, kid,' said John. 'It's the property of the Derbyshire Constabulary now.'

'But I paid for it.'

Technically, Carl had paid for it, but I wasn't going to point that out.

'It's been seized,' said Spong. 'You can't have that original copy.'

'What do you mean original copy?'

'Well…' Spong went behind the TV set and lifted up a second video player.

'You done us a copy?' I asked.

'Yes,' said Spong. 'Did it earlier this evening.'

'No way!'

He smiled. 'Sure have.'

'How much?' asked Paul, his voice sharp.

Spong looked at him. 'No charge. Call it a sorry for how things went down yesterday.'

'And for how much of a cockend your brother is,' said Benton.

'So we can't have the box?' asked Paul.

'No. Sorry.'

Mark said to Paul, 'I hardly think that matters.'

Spong grabbed a tape from the top of the TV and came over to Paul and me and handed it to us. Paul took it.

'Thank you,' I said.

'No worries,' said Dan Spong. 'This could be the end of a very short lived era. I grew up on horror films... sci-fi films... what-have-you. But if the government have their way, films like this...' he waved his arms across the unit, 'will be gone. The evangelical are getting away with murder. They are deceiving the nation, and people are falling for it... in their droves. It's scary. But there has to be critical voices in all this mess, like your friend said.

'I joined the police force to uphold the law, but we're vilifying the wrong people. People like your mate Ray Ellis. Now I have to do my job... or be seen to be doing my job. I am toeing the line... a lot of us on the force are, but that doesn't mean we're happy about it. We are being played by Whitehouse and all her lot, and especially by the media. They are perpetuating this firestorm. For every film we seize and have to destroy, I... sorry, we,' motioning to Benton and the Toad, 'make sure copies are made and we trickle them back out into the world. So this *Evil Dead* is yours. Make sure it never gets lost.'

'We will,' I said.

66.

And just like that, we had a copy of *The Evil Dead*.

67.

So we headed back in the direction of town, this time taking the road and not going via the old train buildings. Me and Paul were buzzing off our new video. Paul held it to his chest like a talisman. Mark remained subdued, hardly saying a word.

Derby Cathedral was lit up by floodlights; a beacon on the skyline of that old Midland town of mine. Paul wanted to go back to his and watch *The Evil Dead* immediately and I was with him on that score. He asked Mark if he had any money left for a taxi and Mark returned a very sharp 'No'. For once, Paul knew better than to say anything else.

We walked in silence for a spell, heading into Iron Gate, the Cathedral towering above us. At the top of Sadler Gate, Mark stopped.

'What's up?' asked Paul.

Mark didn't answer him for a moment, simply stared off down Sadler Gate. Then, he said, 'I've gotta go and see Lindsay.'

'What... now?' said Paul. 'It's well late.'

'So?' said Mark.

'Paul might be right,' I ventured. 'Might be better to go with a clear head tomorrow. She'll probably be in bed anyway.'

'I don't give a shit if she's in bed,' he said. 'I've got to see her.'

I looked at Paul and he shrugged. Then Paul said, 'What about *The Evil Dead*?'

Mark looked at him, a steady rage boiling. Then he said, 'Fuck you, Mansell. All you've got in your head is these fuckin' videos. The both of you have. You need to wake up. This is real life.'

He stormed off down Sadler Gate. I looked at Paul; he rolled his eyes. We both followed Mark.

As we passed the Blue Note, I started to feel sick.

68.

I could hear Mark banging on the Batcave door, calling Lindsay's name. Paul and I were out on the street, looking decidedly uncomfortable. Above, the clouds had rolled on and I could see the Big Dipper, though the moon owned the night.

'Maybe we should leave him to it 'un go back to mine?'

I thought about it. 'We better hang on... just in case she gives him the blow out again.'

'Suppose,' said Paul, and began to kick at the kerb.

The banging and shouting stopped abruptly and I heard Lindsay shout, 'What the fuck are you doing? It's nearly three in the morning!'

'Here we go,' said Paul.

I peered down the narrow passageway that led to the Batcave, but I couldn't see anything. Lindsay's door was off to the side and couldn't be seen from the street. I could hear them though. Loud and clear.

Mark was saying that he needed to talk to her, that he would change, and that he was sorry, and Lindsay said that he didn't even know what he was sorry for and Mark carried on babbling about 'changing' and Lindsay said that they could talk about it in the morning and not in the middle of the night and they went round like this for a good while. Paul sighed and kicked a can across the street.

I heard Lindsay say, 'Who's that?' and Mark told her that it was me and Paul. This didn't impress her in the slightest. 'Fuck sake,' she said. 'You lot all joined at the hip or something...'

'Look, Linz, don't worry about them. Let's go inside and talk.'

'There's nothing to talk about.'

This must have cut Mark because he suddenly fell silent. Paul huffed and leaned on the bonnet of a battered old Opel Rekord. I saw a shooting star and kept it to myself. I wished on it.

Then I heard Lindsay's door shut and Mark didn't return.

'He must've gone inside,' I said.

'Fuck me,' said Paul. 'We could be 'ere ages.'
'We'll give him five more minutes.'
A big mistake.

69.

The next thing I knew Mark was storming down the passageway shouting my name. I backed into the road. Lindsay was running up behind Mark shouting for him to 'Stop!' but Mark ignored her and spat out, 'Bradley, you're dead!'

Paul looked at me in utter confusion. Mark came running up the steps to pavement level and headed straight for me.

'Mark! Wait!' cried Lindsay.

I ran around a car on the other side of the road. My chest felt tight. Mark said, 'You got off with my girlfriend?'

I didn't say anything at first.

Paul looked at me and said, 'What the fuck?'

'Well?' pressed Mark.

'It was a mistake,' I implored. 'I'm sorry.'

'You fuckin' will be.'

Both Mark and Lindsay were out in the road now, Lindsay dragging on his arm, pulling him back. Paul moved away from the Opel Rekord and hung on the edge of the fray, watching the scene unfold.

Mark was staring at me. He looked really pissed. But there was more than just anger there; he looked hurt. Really hurt.

'Mark, I'm so sorry, mate,' I offered again. To my own ears, I sounded utterly pathetic.

'How could you?'

I had no answer.

Lindsay was saying, 'Mark, come back inside...' but Mark took no notice of her. She said, 'It was just a stupid mistake. It meant nothing.'

I looked at her, cut to ribbons, and saw there was indeed nothing for me in her eyes.

I blurted out, 'Why did you tell him?'

She looked away.

Mark cut in, 'Oi! You don't get to talk to her. Not ever again, you hear? You're fuckin' dead to me, Scott.'

Something about the way he used my first name really put the knife in, and I had to choke back tears.

I noticed Paul staring at me and I had to turn away from

him and hide my face. Then I heard Paul say to Mark, 'Mate, she dumped you earlier…'

I looked back at him, stunned. Lindsay went ballistic.

'Fuck you, Mansell!' she screamed. 'You fucking stay out of it.'

'Well,' he dared, 'you got off with Bradley as well…'

She went for him and Paul scurried round the other side of the Opel Rekord. Mark grabbed hold of Lindsay and was now keeping her at bay.

So now there was Paul and I cowering behind cars on either side of the street and the two of them stumbling about in the middle of the road. I may have found it comical if I hadn't felt so utterly wretched. I glanced at the moon and told myself that I was just dust.

Mark looked from me to Paul and back again and said in a low voice, 'You're supposed to be my mates.'

I closed my eyes and swallowed hard.

Lindsay looked up at him and said, 'Let's go inside.'

For a moment I thought he would. All was still. But then he broke away from Lindsay, tore round the car and was on me in seconds. He dragged me out into the road and I heard Lindsay screaming and the scuffing on tarmac and Mark's heavy breathing and my own pounding heart.

He didn't hit me; he simply pushed and pulled me around, snapping my neck back, disorientating me. Then I heard Paul shouting, 'Get off him!' and more tangled arms and scuffling feet, and Lindsay was shouting, 'You three are pathetic,' and I wondered if I agreed with her. Then, somehow, I fell away from the tussle and watched as Mark pushed Paul and the videotape went flying into the air.

70.

We all looked up.

When I think back to it now, I remember it in slow motion.

Like a film.

The tape went end over end, high above us, then it slowed, gravity taking its hold, and brought it back down to earth.

Someone shouted, 'Grab it!' – I'm not sure who; it may have even been me –and I watched it fall towards us and then I leapt into the air.

I went straight across the bonnet of the Opel Rekord and came down in a crumpled heap on the pavement beyond. I looked up and saw the moon and then the faces of my friends were peering down at me.

'You okay?' asked Mark.

'Think so,' I said.

I looked down and saw the videotape clutched to my chest.

71.

I stood up. Paul offered a steadying hand. I gave him the tape and stepped towards Mark. Lindsay was stood behind him, avoiding my eye.

I said, 'Mark. I am sorry. It should never have happened. You can knock me the fuck out if you want – it's what I deserve. I don't give a shit anymore…'

He blinked several times. I felt more tears readying to fall. 'I'm just sick of feeling like this,' I said. 'Like nothing.'

'How can I ever trust you again?' Mark asked.

I looked at him, and at Lindsay, then back at Mark again. 'You won't,' I said.

I knew I'd lost them both.

72.

Mark and Lindsay got married in the summer of 1985. Paul and I weren't invited to the wedding. They had a few kids and moved to Ashbourne. Mark still works in construction. I saw him a few months ago when I was back from a film shoot. We went for a beer and talked about the old days. He seemed good. I was happy for him.

He told me he never did see *The Evil Dead*.

73.

I watched *The Evil Dead* in the early hours of that morning round at Paul's house. We didn't talk much about what had happened. In fact, we didn't say much of anything at all. I think we were both shell-shocked from the events of the past couple of days. I know I was.

We each cracked open a beer – it tasted dreadful – and watched the ultimate experience in gruelling terror. I could hardly believe I was finally seeing it.

74.

The Evil Dead was everything I wanted it to be.

75.

I left Paul's house at around seven. The morning had a fine mist shrouding the streets; the rising sun like a white halo over rooftops. A new day.

Something had fixed in my mind as I'd watched *The Evil Dead*. A clear sense of who I was and what I wanted to do with my life. I knew I would start writing that day and that I was prepared for the winding roads my ambition would lead me down.

I came to stand before my house. The street was quiet and I looked about. This town, these streets, were all that I was, but on that mist-covered morning, I knew I was on the threshold of the next chapter of my life.

I knew the future was wide open.

Andrew David Barker was born in Derby, England in 1975, and has had pretty much every job going. He has worked as a window fitter, a rail track worker, a factory worker, a carpet salesman, a car valeter, a delivery driver, a bricklayer's labourer, a shop assistant, and a care worker, among others. None of them stuck.

In the late 90s he played lead guitar in a rock band. They got signed, made a single, played London, thought they were famous, and, subsequently, imploded. He then turned his hand to filmmaking, accumulating in the little seen opus, *A Reckoning* – a last man on earth tale which won acclaim from many who saw it. His debut novel, *The Electric*, a supernatural, coming of age ode to movies and growing up in the eighties, was first released in 2013. He now lives in Warwickshire with his wife and daughter.

He is, of course, a huge fan of *The Evil Dead*.